Messages From

GOD

Dorothy Mattingly

ISBN 978-1-64416-024-4 (paperback)
ISBN 978-1-64416-025-1 (digital)

Christian Faith Publishing, Inc.
832 Park Avenue
Meadville, PA 16335
www.christianfaithpublishing.com

Printed in the United States of America

DEDICATION AND ACKNOWLEDGEMENT

First of all, this book is dedicated to *My Lord and Savior*, without whom these messages would not be possible.

I would also like to acknowledge the people who have encouraged and supported me in my walk with the *Lord. My* wonderful husband Joe, who has always made sure I had my quiet time with the *Lord.* I would like to thank my mom for always saying: "Keep hanging on."

Lastly and most precious is my sister in the *Lord*, Georgia. With her guidance and assurance, she kept me going. She was always there when I need an answer to a question or to explain a scripture. She has been a mentor to me throughout all my writing.

My Testimony

I've been a Christian for over twenty-five years, visited other churches and participated in praise and worship. I am a member of Trinity Assembly of God and serves in many capacities including serving as a board member, helping others in need, also giving time and personal finances and possessions to those less fortunate than myself, attending church services sitting quietly in the pew three times a week or more during times of revival. I have worked about thirty to forty years cleaning houses, offices, churches, and funeral homes. After retirement, I started having breathing problems around home and decided to see my doctor. One visit lead to a referral to other doctors and a lot of tests. After all the tests, the diagnosis was restricted lung disease which means my lungs don't produce oxygen for the actions of my body. I am now on oxygen 24/7. After some research online, I discovered there is no cure or medicine that will heal me other than a lung transplant or a miracle. I'm praying for that miracle. Like any life-threatening disease, the actual effects didn't sink in until one night while lying in bed trying to go to sleep; I was praying and crying out to the *Lord*. I was asking him, "If I take my last breath tonight and come to *Heaven*, what would *You* say to me?"

The *Lord* said, "*I* know you not." But I reminded the *Lord* of all the good things I had done in *His* name, all the people I had personally helped even taking money from my wallet to give to others.

I said, "*Lord*, I've helped people to pay their utilities bills. *Lord*, *You* knew me before I was born."

Again *He* said, "*I* know you not." I was devastated and hurt. The next morning when I looked in the dictionary for the meaning of to know, I found three meanings. Everyone understands what the word means. What the *Lord* wanted me to understand is this: All the years of reading and studying the Holy Bible, I knew of *Him*, about *Him*, but did not know *Him*. So this is why *He* said *He* didn't know me because I didn't have a relationship with *Him*. So deciding to rectify the situation, I decided to start spending time with the *Lord*. Every morning for the last three years, I have been spending quality time with the *Lord* in worship, devotions, prayer, and Bible study. Then the *Lord* started giving me messages for all people. At first, they were sentences and then paragraphs and finally entire messages. The *Lord* has been gracious enough to give me hundreds of messages and warnings for *His* people. I've learned from all the messages that the main point the *Lord* wanted from *His* people is for them to get and develop a closer relationship with *Him* in these last days. Also, some of the messages are meant to teach and help individuals to live a righteous life in these perilous times. *He* is concerned for those that are lost. It's my desire that these precious words from *God* will help, encourage, and enlighten all people from all nations.

His faithful servant,
Dorothy Mattingly

JANUARY 1, 2016

*M*y people, doing good deeds will not earn your way to *Heaven*. You do good deeds for others, thus showing the love of the *Father*. You cannot earn your salvation. It was given freely many years ago. When will *My* people understand the free gifts *I* have given? Go *My* people and do the will of your *Father* in *Heaven*. Show the lost of the world that by the grace of their *Lord*, they are brought to salvation, not by works. Yet the good deeds they do will bring glory to *God*. They are representing the *Father* on earth by doing *His* will, which is to show the love of the *Lord Jesus Christ*. No amount of good deeds will earn you anything except praise from the receivers. You are saved by grace and the love of *God*. Start the New Year off right by going to the lost people of your world and teach them of the grace of *God*. Tell them of *His* mercy and salvation if they will accept what has been freely given.

JANUARY 2, 2016

*M*y children, come and abide with *Me* for a while. Gather around at the foot of *My* throne. *I* have a story to tell you about a baby. It started long ago. An angel came to a virgin and told her that she had been chosen to bear the *Son of God.* Upon giving *Him* birth, she was to call *Him Emmanuel* (*God* with us). *He* grew up in a loving home. As *He* matured, *He* knew that *He* had to be about *His Father's* business. As *He* grew into manhood, *He* knew that *He* had things to accomplish. *He* went about *His Father's* business. *He* healed many, delivered many from curses, and spoke to many of the coming of the *Messiah. He* had many followers, and yet Satan crept into one of *His* disciples who then betrayed *Him.* This young man named *Jesus* was crucified on a cross for all mankind. *He* gave *His* life that all might be saved. So why are you still waiting? Why not accept what was freely given many years ago? What are you waiting for? Don't wait until the last moment; it may be too late!

JANUARY 4, 2016

Behold, *My* children, do not get caught up with all the things happening in your world. The enemy will use any temptation to pull you away from *Me.* He will make small suggestions to do, say, or act like the people of the world, but you are not of this world. You may live in this world, but you are not of this world. Do not let the enemy get a foothold in your life. Listen to your *Spirit,* man, as to what to do. Test your thoughts and suggestions and see if they line up with *My Holy Word. My* children, you are all human and will fall. It's what you do after you fall that's most important. Seek *Me*! Remember, you have an advocate with the *Father in Heaven.* Humble yourselves and seek *Me.*

JANUARY 5, 2016

Brethren, do you count yourselves followers of the *Lord Jesus Christ*? Are you totally committed to *Him*? You cannot be counted among *My* people and still follow after the things of the world. The worldly things are for a little while, yet heavenly things are for eternity. *My* followers are not drunken with wine but only with the *Holy Spirit*. They speak not harshly of others but speak kindness and encouragement. They do not pick and choose whom they will show love but show love to all *God's* creations. *My* people are not racists; they love everyone regardless of race or religion. In doing this, you are revealing your *Father* to the lost of the world. Followers of *Mine* will consider others before themselves. They will help those in need no matter what the need. They will be respectful of all in authority, remembering that *God* placed those in their positions. If you don't approve of the individuals over you, pray for them daily. You can call yourself a follower of *Mine* when you show your little light and the love of your *Heavenly Father*.

JANUARY 6, 2016

Christians, unlike the days of old when man was head of his household, today's household is headed usually by a single parent. The children of your generation are not being taught biblical principles but by all the things of the world. In turn, they have no respect for their elders. In times of old, children and grandchildren took care of their aging parents. In your busy lives today, adults can't even take care of their children. Man has lost his ability to be head of his household. It's been taken away by all the rights of others. It seems, at one point or another, when making a decision, you will be stepping on someone else's rights. Christian homes should have Christian values. Everyone has rights; it's how they use those *God*-given rights that's important. Individuals have taken the right issues all out of proportion. As Christians, you have a *God*-given right to speak up for what is right and speak against what is wrong. Men, take back what the enemy has taken from you. Become what you were created for—godly men who are not afraid to speak the truth. Take back your rights as Christians.

JANUARY 7, 2016

*M*y children, *I* have bestowed many gifts to all *My* chosen ones. They are peace, joy, grace, mercy, and most of all love for their fellow man. How you use these *God*-given gifts reflect who you are in the *Lord*. The greatest gift of all is love for *I am love*. What your world needs now is more *love* not hatred, rebellion, discontentment, and/or sympathy. Even amongst the Christians, they don't show love to all. When you accept *My* plan of salvation, that makes you a child of the living *God*. Yet some think that if individuals don't come to their house of worship and belong to another church that they are lesser of a Christian. *Not so!* When anyone accepts *Me* as their *God* and *Savior*, they belong to the kingdom of *God*. You are all *My* children regardless of what church you attend! Love all the brethren when and wherever you see them. You are all brothers and sisters in the *Lord*. If there's not love among all *My* children, how then can they show love to others? Take inventory of your thoughts and feelings for others. What the world needs now is love, not hypocrites!

JANUARY 9, 2016

My daughter, why are you concerning yourself about your loved one? Did you not know *I* am still in control? Sometimes *My* people are needful of instructions. The only way they will listen is if everything is taken away and they have no one except *Me*. Sometimes your loved ones get so wrapped up in the worldly things, they forget the path *I* had laid out for them. Your loved one listened to others and got trapped in her own sin. There is a way out. Only she can make the choice. Long ago, she received a prophetic word. It seemed foreign to her as a child. Yet she never pursued its meaning; instead she ran to the world for answers. They were wrong. Your loved one has to hit bottom because then there is only one way out. That's up! When you feel so low and helpless, that's when to call on *Me*. *I'm* always here waiting for them to cry out to *Me*. Pray continuously for all your loved ones.

JANUARY 11, 2016

To all *My* followers, rejoice and count yourselves worthy of the kingdom of *God* if you are shunned, ridiculed, harassed, and even made fun of because you've chosen to follow after *Me*. In this life, you will suffer many trials and afflictions because you have chosen *Me* instead of the worldly things. Remember, *I* suffered many things for you. Don't get drawn into the things the world has to offer. The things of the world are meant to draw and separate you from *Me*. Don't allow it! Come against anything that doesn't pertain to *Me* and *My Holy Word*. You have to live among these people listening to their comments. Let them see that you don't participate in idle words. Only listen to the thoughts that are good and helpful. The enemy will use anything to draw you away from spending time with *Me* and *My Word*. Take control and come against it. Use your armor daily by putting it on in the morning. Protect yourselves from idle comments that are harmful to others. Don't participate in them. Remember to seek after your heavenly rewards, not the rewards of men.

JANUARY 13, 2016

*M*y chosen ones, stay in *My Presence* continually. It's by being in *My Presence* and seeking *My* help and guidance that you will be able to accomplish the plans *I* have for you. It's in *My Presence* that you can relate your problems to *Me*. It's in *My Presence* you should long to be, no matter what you are facing. It's in *My Presence* the problems of the world will seem to disappear. They won't seem so important! It's in *My Presence* you will find peace and contentment. In *My Presence*, you can find everything. So *My* chosen ones, what are you waiting for? Seek *My Presence* and learn about your *Father's* heart. Come into *My Presence*, *My* chosen ones, if only for a little while. *I'm* waiting for you! Accept *My* invitation!

JANUARY 14, 2016

To all the lost souls of the world, *I* have given to you *My* plan of salvation. *My Son* came in human form to deliver mankind from sin. *He* was sacrificed on the cross for your sins. Why then have you not accepted *My* plan for salvation? Lost souls of the world, what are you waiting for? Does it take a catastrophe, an illness, or the loss of a loved one? Why wait until trials and tribulations? Come calling upon *Me*. *I* am willing and able to listen to all who call upon *My* name in their time of need. *I* am always here to help *My* people whenever they call upon *Me*. The lost will only call upon *Me* in their time of need or in an emergency. Why can't they see the need for *Me* in their daily life? Moreover, the blessings that they would receive includes joy, peace, love, and belonging to the kingdom of *God*. Wake up, people, and see your need for a *Savior* before it's too late!

JANUARY 15, 2016

Christians, seems like everywhere you turn there's some new rule or regulation to follow! *I've* commanded *My* people to obey the laws of the land, unless they go against *My Word*. Laws and rules and regulations are supposed to help an individual, yet sometimes they can harm you too! Remember *My* commandments to love your neighbor as yourself. The greatest commandment of all is to *love* the *Lord* your *God* with all your heart, soul, mind, and strength. If the laws of the land would embrace and follow this commandment, your world would be a better place to reside in. *My* creations were created for *love*, but as with Cain, evil has taken hold. Why can't people see the need for a much higher authority and better laws? They need less hatred against each other. Be waiting, *My* people, for one day all these will pass. You should be looking forward for that day when *I* come again for *My* bride.

Christians, are you saddened by all the violence, hatred, racism, and the slaying of the innocent people in your world? Have you prayed, prayed, and prayed, yet it seems nothing gets any better? It's time for all *My* people to take a stand and say, "Enough is enough!" It will take all Christians all over the world to stand firmly together and say, "We are going to do something about this situation." Dedicate a day, an hour for all Christians regardless of faith to stand firm and declare the enemy has been defeated! *He* can only harm *My* people if they sit back and do nothing. Speak the blood of the *Lamb* over your homes, children, families, churches, and your nation. Refuse to back down! Pray on this special day all day long. Everyone must be in agreement and be faithful in doing so. Those who are able to fast, do so. Some, because of medical reasons, cannot participate. Those who can't fast, let them be in continual prayer. Don't let up! No matter where you are at work, at school, at home, wherever you can, pray in your thought life. It will take togetherness and for all to be in agreement. Then you will see results. Be faithful in all you do!

JANUARY 18, 2016

a.m.

Child of *Mine*, just as your prodigal child is in the process of returning to the kingdom, rejoice! That's the excitement and pleasure *I* feel when one of *My* sons and daughters return to the fold after falling away. All the angels in *Heaven* are rejoicing about this revelation. Be vigilant in prayer and thanksgiving. *I* am always in control! Sometimes it may not seem as though *I'm* doing anything. That's when *I'm* working the hardest. Do not be dismayed. *I* will work gently with your loved one. This child has been hurt drastically and needs a lot of healing. *I* will be working ever so gently until *I* bring her back to the path that *I* had chosen for her long ago. This child had to suffer many things before she saw the need for *Me*. It has been a hard lesson, one that will stay with her forever. This has been a fearful and learning experience which *I* will have use to her advantage later. Keep praying for all your loved ones and all the prodigals.

p.m.

Am *I* not the one who created and formed you? Am *I* not the *God* of the whole world? Then why do you fret so? *I* have everything under control! No need for *My* saints to concern themselves, but with *My* help, we can change everything. Remember, nothing is impossible for *Me*! So many of Christians think with small problems, they are best handled by themselves. *My* saints forget that *I'm* the *God* for all your problems, big and small. *I* care about everything that concerns *My* children. As a child of *Mine*, the first thing you need to do is to seek *Me* in prayer. Listen and *I* make known the answers to your concerns. Be open-minded and listen closely to what the *Spirit* is saying to you. Come, *My* children, to the quiet place we share. Seek *Me* above all else, and *I* will make *Myself* known to you, the one who created you. Listen to *My* voice! Shut out all the worldly distractions and be still and know that *I* am *God*.

Child of *Mine*, you come before *Me* with worship and studying *My* Holy Scriptures. You proceed to read all your devotionals about *Me*, and then you sit patiently waiting for *Me* to speak to you. *I* have a message for all *My* people. Why can't you, child of *Mine*, devote a few precious moments in *My Presence* just waiting. It's the desire of *My* heart that all *My* precious children would choose *Me* above all else and come and sit in *My Presence*. By doing so means that they have chosen *Me* above the things of the world. Make *Me* number one in your life. Put all your faith and trust in *Me*. *I* am your friend and will always be with you even until the end of time. Come, *My* children, and hear what *the Word* of *God* is saying. *My* arms are open wide to gather *My* children like a hen gathers her chicks. You will find comfort in *My Presence*, so come and behold *My* glory!

JANUARY 20, 2016

*M*y children, it pleases *Me* when *I* see *My* children choosing to spend quality time with *Me* and sit in *My Presence*. How wonderful it would be in your world if all *My* chosen ones would take the time to sit for a while with *Me*. Life would be so peaceful and joyful. Yet with all the events they participate in their lives, they choose them above all else. When, *My* children, will you take a moment and sit quietly in *My Presence*? In doing so, you would be able to go about your daily routine with a different outlook. It is the desire of *My* heart for all *My* children to come and sit for a moment and lean on *Me* and trust *Me*. Confide in *Me* what's in your heart. *I* know and see all, yet *I* want *My* chosen ones to tell *Me* about their trials and tribulations. They seek advice from others and forget to seek *Me* for advice. *I* am your *Heavenly Father* and possesses more love than the world has ever seen. *I* will guide you in the path of life. Let *Me* guide you in everything you choose. Come and abide with *Me*.

JANUARY 21, 2016

Sons and daughters, while residing in your world going from place to place, when encountering others, begin a conversation with them. Let them see compassion and real caring toward them. Ask them if they were to die this day, where would their soul spend eternity? Some will say, "When you're dead, that's all there is." Explain that their body will return to dust from which it was made, but the soul or spirit is alive and will go to *Heaven* or hell. This is depending on the individual's life and how they lived it. Some you encounter don't even believe in life after death or anything else. Tell them of the great power of *God* and that *He* created all things including trees, birds, and animals. All things seen by human eyes was created by the one true *God*. The *God* of the whole universe. Next, you can tell them of *My* plan of salvation. In this plan upon acceptance, it includes eternity with the one true *God* of the entire world. Seek *My* sons and daughters; go into your world and look for the lost. Bring them into the kingdom of *God*. *I* am waiting patiently for all who will come.

My followers, you've heard the song "Let Your Little Light Shine!" You, *My* chosen ones, are the light, so let your light shine for all to see. Whenever you go, let your light shine brightly so others will say, "There's a follower of the *Lord Jesus Christ*." Don't mask your brightness under a basket. Be bold, and let all see the glory of your *Savior*. Let your face glow with the radiance of your love for the *Lord*. Let your mouth smile with thankfulness. Speak words of kindness, blessings, and wisdom. Let your eyes see all the goodness of others. Your thoughts should be of your *Heavenly Father*. Let your ears hear what the *Spirit of the Lord* is saying to all mankind. Tell others of the *Lord's* love and mercy so they, too, can shine in the knowledge of their *Savior*. Your light is the indwelling of your *Lord* living inside of you, so let your light shine brightly for all to see. Show it to the world, and *let your little light shine!*

JANUARY 23, 2016

Brethren, in your time of need, whom do you seek? Do you call upon the name of *Jesus*, or do you seek someone else? *My* people, *I* am always here in your hour of need. Just call out *My* name, and *I* will hear you. Brethren, you know that you don't have to wait for trouble to call out *My* name! Because you are *Mine*, you can call on *Me* 24/7. *I* am always here waiting for you to use *My* name. There's power in the name of *Jesus*, so use it anytime when the need arises. Call out to *Me* for all your needs, even the smallest ones. *My* brethren, you have chosen to follow after *Me*, and then let *Me* be your advocate and problem solver. *I* will never leave you or forsake you. Stay on the path *I* have set before you, and when trials and tribulations come, call out *My* name, *Jesus*. *My* name is more powerful than any other, so use it when anything comes against you. *I* have given to all *My* followers the authority to use *My* name!

JANUARY 25, 2016

*M*y people, *I* talk to you, *My* people, daily, yet your minds are cluttered with the things of your world that it blocks out what *I* wish to say. Unclutter your thoughts and your life. *My* people have put themselves in a prison of their own making. *I* come to break the bonds that bind, *My* people, and set them free. Set your thoughts on *Me*, and *I* will help you unclutter your mind that's being held captive with all the things in your life. When you set your thoughts on *Me* and put *Me* in control, you will soon see freedom. Then you will be able to hear what the *Spirit of the Lord* is saying to *His* people. Come to *Me* with open heart and mind by putting your trust and faith in *Me*.

JANUARY 26, 2016

Just as some days are dark, dreary, and overcast, people in the world living in sin view their life this way with no hope in sight. Then when a ray of sunshine peaks through the clouds, they rejoice because it gives them a ray of hope. You, *My* people, as Christians can be that ray of sunlight to the lost world. Let the lost see your light shining brightly. You, *My* people, are the ones to lead the lost to the pathway of salvation. Let your light shine and show the lost ones there's hope. It is in the *Lord Jesus Christ*. So, *My* people, in this overcast world of sin, let the lost see in you the awesome presence of the *Lord* residing in you. Tell them they can have the same by accepting the *Lord* as their *Savior*. If only this world would see that *I, Son of God*, am the only hope for this lost generation. *I* am the light and hope for all mankind. *I* say to the lost souls that are depressed and feel alone, "Come unto *Me* and accept *My* salvation, and *I* will give you peace, not as the world knows but everlasting peace and comfort for those who invite *Me* into their hearts."

My chosen people, seek *Me* and *My* wisdom and guidance in everything that you do. Don't be misled by meaningful friends. Sometimes they may give you information that does not line up with *My Word*. It's up to *My* people to know the Scriptures so they won't be misled. Listen to people and like the saying, "Take everything with a grain of salt so are their words until they are backed up by *My Word*."

There are pastors and ministers that are teaching false doctrines. It's up to *My* people with the spirit of the living *God* to determine what is true and what is false. Pray about all things, seeking *Me* and *My Word* in all matters. Make sure to line everything up with *My Word*. In this sinful world, it's hard to believe in mankind. You can always put your trust in *Me* and *My Holy Word*. *I* do not lie, nor do *I* ever change. *I* am the same yesterday, today, and tomorrow.

My people should be aware of false teachings all around them. It's up to them to know *the Word of God* so they can discern what is true and that it lines up with *My Word*.

JANUARY 28, 2016

My saints, do you not know it's better to give than to receive? Are you givers or receivers? If givers, then give out of the abundance of blessings *I* have given to you. Being a receiver means you receive the things of *God* and pass them on to others. Sometimes receivers are like hoarders; they receive and keep it for themselves instead of passing it on. The blessings *I* give to *My* saints are to be shared with all that will receive it. Being givers, you should give of yourselves time, help, and finances to all those in need. This means even in your houses of worship, if there is someone in need. The widows, widowers, and single-parent households in the church if they don't have anyone, it's up to the other saints to help them. Let it be known that you are willing and able to help those in need.

Maybe someone just needs a good listener or a prayer of faith. Just be a friend to those in need. Then you will receive blessings from those that you have helped. You will also receive your heavenly rewards.

JANUARY 30, 2016

*M*y dear saints, when ministering to the lost, do it with love and gentleness. Let them see humbleness and humility when you are reaching out to them about *the Word of God*. Some of you, without realizing what you are doing, become forceful in desiring to witness to the lost. Share with all the love of your *Father* in *Heaven*. You do this with meekness and humble of spirit. What the lost is suffering from is the lack of love and understanding. The world they live in is so busy; it doesn't have time to help those in need. Be very compassionate and patient when it comes to ministering to the lost. Sometimes it is just someone to take the time to listen. By listening, you will be showing the love and compassion of your *Father* in *Heaven*. *My* people should possess a humble spirit in all they do and say. What the world needs is love, the real love of a *Savior*!

FEBRUARY 1, 2016

My people, there's battles raging all around you. You must pick your battles very carefully. Put on your full armor and declare the name of the *Lord* because you are *My* people. There will be continual battles all around. As *My* people, you are equipped with the weapons of warfare. You have been given from within. It's called the *Holy Spirit*. *He* will lead you in all your battles or dealings with the enemy. As *My* people, you will be tried and tempted. Take heart, *I* have overcome the world. The battle has already been won. You must declare this daily in your own life. Speak it out loud so there won't be any misunderstanding. Declare to the enemy whether it be health issues, finance, whatever the need that *I* have defeated *Him* at Calvary, and *He* has no hold on *My* people, only if they allow it. Stand up, *My* people, and start declaring the blood of *Jesus* and the name of the *Lord* in all the land. Be bold and brazen in this declaration. Say, "Greater is *He* that is in me than he that is in the world. With *God* on my side, who can come against me?"

To all *My* ministers, yes, all those who speak or witness to the lost are called ministers of *the Word of God*. Be on the alert, *My* chosen ones, and set examples for all others to follow. Don't get involved in meaningless discussions. Do not get too involved in the things of your world unless it pertains to your faith then, *My* people, stand firm. *My* people can often be pulled into a discussion of worldly matters and then realize that the views are different than *the Word*. Judge all views and standards by *the Word of God*. It does not change, and *I* do not change. I'm the same yesterday, today, and forever. Do not get caught up in trivial matters that lead to nowhere. Be vigilant, honest, and true to your beliefs. Take heed all who minister *the Word of God* by being what *I* have called you to do. Stay in *the Word*.

February 3, 2016

*M*y people, *I* tell you, *My* people, to give *Me* all your cares and worries! Why then don't you understand when you give something to another, give it completely, no holding back? *My* people should have enough faith and trust in *Me* to allow *Me* to deal with all their cares. *I* don't need any help, yet *My* people want to keep being involved in the circumstances. That's saying that they don't believe that *I*, the *Creator* of the universe, can solve or take care of their problems. Some of *My* people don't get answers to their problems because they are in the way of an answer. Remove yourself from the equation and release everything to *My* capable hands. Don't be concerned anymore. Give to *Me* completely all your cares and concerns, and *I* will take care of them for your benefit. When you release everything to *Me*, don't take it back! Leave your cares and worries at the altar!

*M*y dear brothers and sisters, I've called you out of darkness into *My* marvelous light. The desire of *My* heart is for all *My* brothers and sisters to be silent no longer, speak up of the atrocities going on in your world. Let your voices be heard. When anything goes against *My Word*, speak out. The evil has become so rampant. *I* have given to you the authority and weapons for warfare. *My* people have become so complacent saying, "*I* can't change anything." Yes, you can. Like a voice crying in the wilderness, it will be heard, but first, you must take a stand and speak up. If all my brothers and sisters would band together (regardless of faith) and declare we are not going to take this anymore, something will change. Come together in prayer. It's not what you choose; it's the togetherness. If all my brothers and sisters take a stand for one day and be faithful, they will see mountains fall and miracles happen!

To *My* followers, enter into a day of rest, *My* people. Let *Me* take your cares, and worry no more! Turn everything over to *Me*. This is a gift *I* give to you. Be free of the worries of this life by turning everything over to *Me*. Put your faith, hope, and trust in the one who created you. Live your life in peace and worry-free. *I* have given to you the gift of rest; accept it and release your cares to *Me*. Rest with the knowledge that *I* will take care of all your worries. You know, worry is a sin! It means that when you worry, you don't believe *I* can do what *I* said *I* would do. Be still and know *I* am *God*! With *God*, all things are possible. If you want a carefree and worry-free life, put all your trust in *Me*.

Children of the *Most High*, sometimes afflictions come your way to teach you humble obedience of *My* will for your life. Just as your earthly parents allow their children to learn from mistakes, *I* sometimes allow afflictions to teach and guide *My* children to be humble in spirit. *My* children cannot be baby Christians and survive in this cruel environment. They have to grow up and learn how to deal with the attacks of the enemy they face daily. The way to grow up for them is to study *My Word*, use it daily. Immature Christians should be humble before *Me* and seek *My* guidance. *I* will not allow more to be put upon them than they can bear. Remember to come into *My Presence* and humble yourselves before *Me* when you can't bear anymore. Come unto *Me*, and *I* will give you rest and comfort. *I* am your *Father in Heaven*. *I* am but a prayer away. Speak, *My* children, your *Heavenly Father* is waiting and listening for *His* children to come to *Him*.

FEBRUARY 8, 2016

My loved ones, once you were lost, and now you've been set free. Freedom came with a huge price. It was the amazing love that *I* have for all mankind that *I* chose to set them free. By setting free all those whom have chosen to follow after *Me*, *I* became their healer, deliverer, constant companion, and friend. *I* as their friend will stick closer than a brother. *I* bore their sins upon the cross and took the stripes on *My* back for healings, yet *My* loved ones don't understand or have not accepted what *I* did for them. It grieves *Me* when *I* see *My* loved ones carrying guilt about some sin they committed or some illness that has been put on them. Remember, *I* hung on the cross to free you from all your burdens. It's up to you, *My* people, to declare that *I* am healed by the blood of the *Lamb* and what *He* did on the cross for me. Tell the enemy that he has no authority or power over you. Tell him that he is a liar and the father of lies. Declare, *My* loved ones, that you are a child of the *Most High God* bought by *His* blood!

FEBRUARY 9, 2016

To all who have ears, let them hear what *the Word of God* is said to *His* people. Behold! *My* chosen ones, the time is now for all *My* people to separate themselves from the people and things of the world. Separate yourselves from among them. Let all who have eyes see the presence of the *Lord* in you. Be silent no longer. Let it be known you are a child of the *Most High God*. The time is now, *My* people, to take back the possession of the things the enemy has stolen from you. Be brazen and bold to the principalities of your world and declare you are taking back everything he has stolen from you. Don't relent! Keep in hot pursuit and make it clear that you will not give in or give up. Some of *My* people have become too laid back and have accepted things and done nothing about them. Don't be comfortable until you get back everything. Say, "In your face, devil, and *I* will be in your face until *I* get everything that you stole from me. *I* am a child of *God* covered by the blood."

FEBRUARY 10, 2016

Rejoice! Rejoice! Rejoice! In the days of old, the priest offered up sacrifices. Now with the new covenant, *Jesus* Christ gave himself as a sacrifice for all mankind. When you become a believer, you are forgiven from all your sins. *Jesus* took all that when *He* went to the cross for you. So, *My* people, rejoice, *I* say, and be glad that the *Lord God* loved you so much that *He* died for you. *I* say again, rejoice! Give *Him* praise, honor, and glory for all the things *He* has done. Rest, *My* people, in *His* peace, love, and forgiveness. Relax in *Him* knowing *He* will take care of everything. It's up to you to trust and put your faith in *Him* and all *He* has done for you. *I* say again, rejoice and come into *His Holy Presence* and see the *Lord* is good.

FEBRUARY 11, 2016

Brethren, in your world of events, there is coming a day when *My* children will celebrate a day for love. On this special day, they give gifts of flowers, sweets, and cards to speak of their love for another. That's nice for couples, but what about the people who are alone? Make a special effort for those that are alone on this day that represents love to show the love of *God* to all. Everyone is loved by the one who created them. Tell them they are not alone that *I* am always there for them with open arms. I'm waiting for all who will come and abide with *Me*. On this day that everyone is celebrating love for another, remember to tell *Me* of your love for *Me*. *I* want all *My* brethren to love everyone; that's the true heart of their *Heavenly Father*.

FEBRUARY 12, 2016

My children, what is faith to you, *My* children? Is it just something you believe in, or is it something you act on? It should be both believed and acted on. Where does your faith lie? Is it in something the world has to offer, or is it eternal? Search, *My* people, your hearts and minds. Faith is believing in something or unseen but believing anyway. Faith believes that *I* am who *I* say *I* am. Believing in the worldly things will only bring grief and destruction. Put your faith in *Me*, the one who knows all who created all in the universe. The *Great I Am*! By faith, you, *My* blessed ones, will see *Heaven*. By prayer and faith, you can come into *My Presence*. In times of old, the high priest offered up sacrifices in the temple for the sins of the people. Today because of *My* sacrifice on the cross, *My* believers can come before *Me* and present their petitions to a *Holy God* by faith. *My* people, you will inherit the kingdom of *God*. Put your faith in the one and only true *God*.

Children of the *Most High*, sometimes being human, you will commit sin. It's then *My Holy Spirit* will convict and convince you to make it right. *He* will continually bring to your memory and thoughts, hoping for you to do what is right. Sometimes *I* will take action and discipline *My* children and show them the right path to follow. With discipline, sometimes it reveals itself as an uncontrollable crying. That's when, *My* children, you are being disciplined by your *Heavenly Father*. Your earthly fathers corrected you when you were wrong. How much more will your *Heavenly Father* correct and guide you? If *I* don't correct you (by *My Spirit*), then you are not *My* children. *I* will correct and discipline all the ones that belong to *My* family. *I* will guide them on the right path of righteousness, if they only will accept *My* direction. *My* children, you will slip and fall; pick yourself up and continue forward. *My* children, *I* will never leave you nor forsake you. If you truly are a child of *Mine*, accept *My* corrections gracefully.

FEBRUARY 16, 2016

My children, pray without ceasing! Pray about everything because when you pray, you are speaking to *Me*. That means that you believe and trust *Me* to handle all your circumstances. When someone hurts you verbally or physically, turn the other cheek. That means not to retaliate or seek vengeance. Come to *Me*, and *I* will administer the punishment those whom have wronged you. "Vengeance is *Mine*," saith the *Lord*. You, *My* children, are to show the love of your *Heavenly Father*. *I* will bless those who bless others. In your conversations, speak only of love when discussing others. Bless those who curse you. Be kind to all, showing the love of your *Father* to all mankind. Remember to pray without ceasing!

FEBRUARY 17, 2016

*M*y people, faith without works is dead. You must possess both. By using your faith, it will produce works; standing on and believing in your faith shows everyone who you are in the *Lord*. By the works of your faith, it will set an example for other people to see and follow; combining the two makes you a true Christian. By faith, you say to the poor, "Be blessed." By works, you then help bless the poor by giving food, clothing, and shelter. Then by sharing your faith with others, it will increase. As you show others works of faith, also show them the plan for salvation.

My people, always think before you speak. Remember that once the words are spoken, they cannot be taken back. Does the power of your tongue need to put in check? You need to let *God* be the master of your tongue. As with a bridle put in the mouth of a horse, it takes a rider holding the reins to guide it. So as with your tongue, it takes *God* to guide it in what it says. Take a moment before speaking to think about what you are to say. Remember, once the words are spoken, they can't be retrieved. So be extremely careful with regards to speech and especially when speaking of others. Good and bad cannot come from the same source. It can only be one or the other. Take heed, *My* people, and watch what you say and be more careful of what is said about others. You are to build others up not tear them down.

FEBRUARY 19, 2016

The things of your world are very tempting. Be strong, *My* chosen ones, and don't get caught up in all those appealing prospects. They are an entrapment to take you away from *Me* (your first love). You cannot be a friend of the world and a friend of *Mine*. Choose this day in whom you will serve. Why can't all the people see what's happening to all mankind? If only they would remove the blinders. *My* people are becoming a slave to the things of the world. People, people, people, be bold and take the authority that has been given to you. State, "No longer will *I* be a slave to the world!" Break the chains, shake them off, and declare, "*I* am a child of the *Most High*. *I* am not taking being pushed around by the enemy and all his worldly things. All *I* need is *the Word of God* in my life and live by it to the best of my ability!"

FEBRUARY 20, 2016

*M*y children, don't limit your worship to just the churches nor limit the taking of Holy Communion to one place. That's putting *Me* in a box and tying *My* hands. I'm everywhere, so you can worship *Me* and take Holy Communion in other places as long as it is done respectfully. By taking communion only in your houses of worships, you are saying that you can only honor *Me* there. You can honor and worship *Me* everywhere. It's like saying that *I'm* only available at the churches. *I* am available whenever *My* children call upon *My* name no matter where they are. *I* am the *God* of everything and everywhere. *I* see all and hear all, so *My* children acknowledge *Me* and proclaim *My* name everywhere!

My followers, there is still some among you who are wavering in their faith. They are led to believe that *I* show favorites in regard to the healings and blessings. *I* am no respecter of persons. *I* will be impartial in *My* dealings with all *My* people. What you, *My* followers, are misunderstanding is why some people are blessed financially and some healed. *I* cannot bless two people the same when one is in obedience and the other is in rebellion. Sometimes it's the attitude of the ones who conform to *My* holiness. All of *My* judgement will be according to every man's work in *My* kingdom.

FEBRUARY 23, 2016

*M*y brothers and sisters, are you seeking after healings? *I* bore your sin and sickness on the cross. You, *My* people, need to accept what has already been done for you. It's up to you to demand from the enemy what has been stolen and take it back. Healing is yours; just receive it by faith and rejoice in it. Don't let anyone tell you any different. Stand on *My Word* which says, "By *My* stripes, you were healed. Believe *My* report and stand on it. On the cross, you were made whole." Claim this daily and rebuke the enemy. He is a liar! Do not give in to his attempts! He will use everything to pull you away from *Me*. It's up to you to declare, "I'm not going to take this anymore. *I* am healed by the blood of the *Lamb* and the word of my testimony. Devil, you have no authority over me. I'm a child of the living *God* and covered by the blood of the *Lamb*."

FEBRUARY 24, 2016

All *My* people, do you want to know *Me* and about *Me*? *I* am just a prayer away. When you really want to know about *Me*, start with your Bible and reading the Holy Scriptures then research. Any questions you may have are found in *My* written *Word*. It's up to you, the individual, to take time in reading and studying *My Word* and what the meaning is and how it speaks to your problem. *The Word of God* speaks to all who will listen. *I* speak all the time to *My* chosen ones who are willing to listen by committing their lives to *Me*. *My* sheep will know *My* voice and be open to what *the Word* is saying. As you take time to read *My Word*, then spend a few moments in *My Presence* talking to *Me* about your daily cares and woes. *I* am a true friend, and *I'm* concerned about all your needs and desires. Come to *Me* and seek *Me* when the going gets rough. *I* will smooth out all the bumps in your pathway of life. Just ask!

*M*y chosen generation, many of you will suffer trials and tribulations, afflictions, persecutions, all because you have chosen to follow *Me* and *My* plan of salvation. Count yourselves worthy because *I* also suffered many things for you. Let these afflictions humble you and bring you closer to *Me*. During your walk of faith with *Me*, the enemy will burden you with many things. Do not bow to *His* temptations. Be strong in your faith and declare to the enemy that the *God* you serve will bring you through the fire, and you won't be burned, no matter how difficult your life may seem. Remember this: You have a mission to do, and you must remain faithful in the *Lord*. *He* will bring you through!

FEBRUARY 27, 2016

Child of *Mine*, are you seeking peace from all your worldly cares? The only place you will find perfect peace is in *My Presence* and *My Word*. The world offers peace, but it's only temporary. *My* peace *I* give to you is eternal, but you must give all your problems to *Me*. Rest in the knowledge that nothing is impossible for *Me*. Peace *I* give to you abundantly, and by accepting, you decide to let *Me* be your problem solver. *I* want to be your everything, your comforter, friend, healer, peace deliverer, protector, and all around your *Heavenly Father*. This is what *I* want for all *My* children. The promises of the things *I* have for you are eternally yours upon request, and then receiving, receive *My* gifts which are freely given to all those that are needful.

FEBRUARY 29, 2016

To all who have ears, let them hear what *the Word of God* is saying! Be aware of all those who teach contrary to *the Word of God*. If the teaching doesn't line up with Scripture, disregard it. Compare all teachings to *the Word*. Read and study *My Holy Scriptures* so as not to be deceived. When someone teaches a message, then you will know what truth is and what's not. The indwelling of *My Holy Spirit* will quicken you to the truth. The only way not to be deceived is to know *the Word of God*. Read and study *My Word* continually. Research the Scriptures. When a verse speaks to your situation, memorize that particular verse. Stand firm on what *the Word* says. By knowing *My Word* and by faith, you will not be misled or deceived. Stay in *My Holy Word*!

My children, yes, you are *My* children when you follow after the things of *My* kingdom. Seek not after the worldly possessions but peace, joy, love, forgiveness, and compassion, which are gifts of *My Spirit*. *My* greatest gift to all *My* children is love for all mankind. There would be peace among you if all *My* children would show love to all *My* creations, just as *I* showed *My* love to you by sacrificing *My Son*. By showing love and kindness to others, you will experience joy unspeakable. It's an emotion that is beyond understanding. Try it and see the beautiful results it will bring. Show a little kindness to all whom you encounter. A small gesture of a smile or a simple hello sometimes breaks the ice for you to start a conversation to this lost and dying world. You be *My* light and shine brightly, *My* children. You are representing your *Father in Heaven*.

MARCH 3, 2016

Child of *Mine*, are you truly children of the *Most High God*? Do you possess love for all *My* creations? Remember, to be truly a follower of *Mine*, you must love with all your spirit, soul, and body. Love is the greatest gift of all time. Everything revolves around love in *My* kingdom. Your love for all mankind is a reflection of *Me* for all to see. *I* am the *God* of love. I've loved you even before time began, so you should show that love to others. By showing the smallest act of kindness to others is an actual act of love. Being considerate and thoughtful of others is in itself an act of love. Let everything you do as a child of *Mine* reflect the love of your *Heavenly Father*. Love never fails; it will always bring blessings, maybe not of this life but in your eternal glory. To be a child of *Mine*, you must possess love for all to see. It's an outward expression of who you are: child of *Mine*.

MARCH 5, 2016

To *My* Child,

You are the total sum of the commandment which says, "Honor thy father and thy mother." You graciously took care of not only your husband until his departure but both of your parents, giving of your time, assistance, and your presence. For years, you patiently nursed your soul mate's needs and care without ever getting or receiving thanks. Your blessings are mounting up in *Heaven.*

In your younger years, you were even taking care of the elderly. Then later you had a family, taking care of your children's needs. Then one day, you decided to make *Me* your *Lord and Savior.* Since then, you have been showing the love of your *Heavenly Father.* Your gift of servitude exceeds all expectations. You've taught your children to help those in need. You have set guidelines and standards for them to follow. When the word *servant* is used, *I* think of you. Your rewards will be great. You have been blessed with many years on earth. One day, you will see *Me* face to face.

Your *Heavenly Father*!

MARCH 6, 2016

Child of *Mine*, you are the apple of your *Father's* eye. You are carrying out *My* plans for you in delivering *My* messages. Give the messages to those that they are intended for. Those individuals will do with them as they choose. Heeding them is to their advantage; disregarding them, to their dismay. Child of *Mine*, by *My* stripes, you were healed! By *My* stripes, you were healed! By *My* stripes, you were healed! Declare this daily. Stand on *My Word*, and make this declaration. *My* child, *I* have given you many messages. Start to use them to benefit others as well as yourself and your family and friends. *I* am your *God*, your healer, your protector, your comforter, your friend, your everything. Look to no one else. *My* promises and blessings are for all *My* loved ones. Do not give up or give in to the enemy. *My* child, apple of *My* eye, *I* have not forsaken nor have *I* forsook you. Tell others of *My* work in you and show them the messages. Put them out there for all to see and learn of *Me* and the plans *I* have for all *My* followers. Also, they need to heed *My* warnings and change the things in their lives that are hindering their relationship with *Me*! By faith, *My* child, you were made whole.

MARCH 7, 2016

*M*y faithful servant, many times in the few last years, you have come before *Me*, faithfully studying and reading *My Holy Word. I* have taught you many things and have spoken many things to you. Pass *My* messages to all who will listen. Those that have ears, let them hear what the *Spirit of the Lord* is speaking to all *His* people. You, *My* faithful servant, are sowing seeds of *My Word* for the harvest. Hopefully they will mature into plants. Sow seeds on fertile ground that has been prepared beforehand. Take notice, *My* child, and be careful. Deliver your messages with the love of your *Father*. Show *My* love to all, passing around *My* love for all to see and behold. *My Spirit* is living in you. Be gentle and do not grieve *Him*! *He* will lead and guide you through your pathway of life. Peace and blessings to all!

To all who are lost, one day, death will come upon you. As you came into the world with nothing, also when you depart this world, you will leave with nothing. Are you prepared for death? There is life after death, whether you believe or not. For those who believe in life after death will have an eternity in *Heaven*. For those who disbelieve will suffer dying over and over again in the lake of fire. It's an eternity of punishment with not a moment of relief. Stop, lost people of the world, and consider this! Upon your death in a blink of your eye, your spirit (soul) leaves your fleshly body. Your body returns to dust from which it came. Your spirit enters one place or another, *Heaven* or hell. For those accepting *My* salvation will enter into *My Presence*, absent from the body and present with the *Lord*. Lost souls, you must decide while you are in your world whom you will serve. Choose wisely. It's your eternal future. Will you choose *My* plan of salvation, or will you remain a slave of the world? The world can't save you! Only *I*, the *Creator*, can give you eternal life.

MARCH 9, 2016

*M*y children, it's *My* heart's desire that all *My* chosen ones will come to know of *Me* and about *Me*. *My* children, do you really know your *Heavenly Father*? Come! *I* say come! *I'm* bidding you to come into *My Holy Presence*. Worship, pray, and seek *My* face. *I* long so for all *My* loved ones to come to the throne room and experience *My* glory. *I* am no respecter of persons. *I* love all *My* creations. Some are more faithful than others and truly want to spend time with *Me*. Some are fly-by nighters. They only seek *Me* during times of need. *I* hear their requests, and *I* am always there for *My* children just as they are always available for their offsprings. This plea *I* have made before, and it seems it needs to be repeated. The things in your world are getting more rushed and busier. The world is racing faster and faster into oblivion. Take heed, and don't let the things going on around you entrap you into that lifestyle. Take time to enjoy the things *I* have given to you, a beautiful sunrise and sunset, gorgeous flowers blooming by the wayside, rivers of living water flowing ever so gently, trees of every kind blowing in a breeze. In your hurried life, you may not notice these gifts. Take the time to stop and smell the roses. Come and spend a little time with *Me* your *Creator*!

MARCH 10, 2016

To all *My* people, say, "Thus saith the *Lord*, 'Come, all *My* people, into the presence of the *Lord*!'" *I* say to those who are burdened and heavy laden, come! To those who are hurting, *I* say come! To any that needs healing *I* say, come! *I* say to those who need deliverance, *I* say come. Yet many of you do not understand *I* am your friend, healer, and deliverer and have the ability to carry all your burdens. Nothing is impossible for *Me*, but first, *My* people, you must seek *Me* for the answer to all their woes. Put your faith and trust in the one who can and will take care of you. *I* will never leave or forsake you. *I* am the *God* of the Bible. Come unto *Me* for everything, and *I* will give you rest, peace, and security. To do so, *I* must be asked. What are you *My* people waiting for?

MARCH 11, 2016

Child of *Mine*, you have cried out and prayed for *My* power. You already possess the power; you were just too meek to use it. *I* will give you the opportunity to pray for others with boldness as you requested. Take heed, *My* child; *I* am with you. *I* will use you in many ways. Just be willing to accept the plans *I* have for you. *My* child, you have been a pew warmer for too long. No longer will you sit quietly by and let others do your work. *I* have been teaching and training you for this purpose. Others may not understand, and still others may be frightened by your demeanor. Tell them not to be alarmed. It's *My Spirit* residing in you. The enemy cannot be fought or defeated with meekness. When you go to war, you are there to do battle. That's accomplished with boldness and authority. *I* am disheartened with *My* children sitting back meekly and letting the enemy put afflictions upon them. Stand up and be bold and say, "We won't take it anymore. Devil, you will restore everything you have taken from me and all my loved ones. *God* is still in control. You, devil, have no power over *God's* children, and they are not going to take it anymore! They are fighting back."

MARCH 12, 2016

*M*y followers, *I* am the *God* of *Heaven* and earth. *I* have conquered death, hell, and the grave. Why then don't *My* followers have enough faith and trust to seek *Me* about their problems? *I* am able and available to conquer and solve all the problems plaguing *My* people. Come, *My* people, and seek *Me* for your healing. Seek *Me* for all your financial needs. Seek *Me* every hour, every minute of the day. *I* am the *God* for all your needs. In these perilous times, *I* am the *God* for all times and all the things! Keep *Me* in all things including your words and deeds. *I* am the *God* who sticks closer than a brother. *I* will never leave you even if you fall away from *Me*. *I* will always be right there to pick you up and welcome you back. *My* people, the way things are happening in your world, the only thing for you to do is stay in fervent prayer. Pray! Pray! Pray! *I* am still in the midst of all situations, and nothing is too hard for *Me*. *I* am in control!

MARCH 14, 2016

My brethren, you are living in perilous times. Things are getting worse in each passing day. Sometimes it may seem like things get worse before actually getting better. Stay in constant prayer with *Me*, and seek *My* advice on all things. Your world is divided, some accepting Christianity while others have taken *God* out of everything. In some places, *My* name cannot even be spoken. Your world is reaping what it has sown for many years, allowing prayer to be taken out of schools and government meetings. Prayer was the covering for such organizations. Now without covering, the people have become evil and have started taking lives, usually the lives of the innocent children. The evil around you can be overcome and defeated if *My* followers will be in prayer and fasting for their nation. Brethren, you need to become bolder and more aggressive in winning the lost. Prayer will overcome the world. *I* have given to you the power of *My Holy Spirit*; use it against the evil ones. Fast and pray against all the evil, if only more of *My* people would begin to fast and pray and stand against the things going on in your nation. All the Christians of the world need to be united in this request. Stand up, *My* people, and be bold and counted among the people of faith.

MARCH 15, 2016

To all *My* people, the world gives you choices, always choices and decisions to the made. Whom will you choose to follow? In selecting a person of authority, listen to their words. Some will say one thing and do something different. Yet others just tell the people what they want to hear. That is called sugarcoating the issues. Any person seeking an authoritative position should be above all else a believer and honest in their dealings with others. In this age, honesty is a commodity that few people behold as a virtue. There are people that will tickle your ears with words pleasing to your understanding. Don't be led astray or deceived. Be alert and on guard, *My* people! In a decision making or a choice to be made, seek *Me* first in prayer. Then wait patiently upon *Me*. Remember, *My* ways and timing are not man's timetable. Your answer will be for coming. It may not be the answer you were seeking, but *I* see what's in your future. *I* know what's best. As long as you live on this earth, there will be choices and decisions to make. Always be guided and led by *My Holy Spirit*.

MARCH 16, 2016

To all *My* followers, *My* people are being persecuted everywhere because of their faith. Innocent babies are being killed by professionals. People are being killed inside and outside their homes, in the streets, and in places of employment. People, you are living in the last days. It seems those in authority continue to allow the persecution of the saints. A *God*-fearing person in authority may help bring about individual's right to worship *God* anywhere without consideration for their welfare. Followers of the *Lord Jesus Christ* should be able to speak of *Me* and about *Me* without being harassed. Freedom is a gift! *I* died so that all *My* people would be free, freedom from all chains of oppression. Yet *My* people are still persecuted. It's up to all *My* followers to say, regardless what the world says, "*I* am a servant of the *Lord Jesus Christ*. *I* will speak *His* name anytime *I* want to no matter who it may offend. *I* will pray openly when given the chance." *My* people, it's time to be bold in the *Lord*; declare we are no longer being pushed in the corner or ignored. We will make ourselves known. The *Lord* says, "*I* am with you always!"

MARCH 17, 2016

To all Christians, why do you spend time and concern yourself with negative people? They will only be won over by the love of your *Heavenly Father*. The time and energy in disapproving their attitudes should be used for *My* benefit. The lost of the world don't understand the qualities of a good and righteous individual. In discussion with anyone, look for the good in them. Your world is in utter chaos. People can't decide which way to turn. Mankind will always let you down. Don't put your complete trust in them, those claiming to be Christ followers. Then they start speaking against the things in *My Holy Word*. Trust only in the *Lord*!

Believers, so much chaos going in your world, people saying one thing and doing another, claiming to be followers of the *Lord* and yet keep changing *My Word* for their own purpose. *My Word* is true and does not change. It is the same yesterday, today, and forever. Believers seek after *Me* and *My Word* of truth. People of your world profess they are Christians yet speak words contrary to the written *Word*. Do not believe or put your trust in such individuals. They will mislead all who follow after them.

Seek *Me* and *My* written *Word*! Put your trust and faith in the one true *God* who does not change and holds the title of *King* of kings. Believers, follow after *Me*. *I* will never leave you nor forsake you. Your world may seem to be in utter chaos with nowhere to turn! Come, *My* people, and put your trust in *Me*. *I* don't waver, nor do *I* lie. Don't be deceived by those who make promises or pledges they can't keep. You, *My* people, have promises from your *Savior*. All you have to do is accept and believe.

MARCH 18, 2016

*M*y chosen ones, *I* have bestowed upon you the same power that rose *Jesus* from the grave. That gift is the *Holy Spirit*. Why, *My* people, are you not using this power? Why are you sitting idly by doing nothing as your world is in chaos? Take authority over the enemy! Declare that *He* has been defeated long ago. Keep commanding this declaration over your nation. Speak it out and don't give up or give in to anything that doesn't line up with *the Word*. *My* people, you are too comfortable with what's going on around you. Stand up and say, "*I* believe in *the Word of God*. *The Word of God* is true, and it will prevail." *The Word* says homosexuality is an abomination. *The Word* says that abortion, no matter the circumstances, is murder. Speak up, *My* people, and let your voices be heard. Unite and declare for all to hear what *the Word of God* is saying.

To all *My* followers of the world, this is to all who are obsessed with all happenings in the world. It's *My* desire that all followers of the Holy Scriptures would be so obsessed with *My Word*. What does worry or concern about events of your world give you? Headaches, heartaches, and depression. Come unto *My* world and experience all freedoms. In *My* worldly kingdom of believers, they have joy unspeakable. They are freed from all earthly woes, leaving all their cares to *Me*, their *Heavenly Father*. They will receive blessings immeasurable. If only *My* followers would realize that only through *Me* can circumstances be changed. It's up to the individuals to seek *Me* for guidance in all things. *I* am the *God* of the big things as well as the little things. Nothing is impossible for *Me*. *I* am only limited by *My* people and what they pray for. Follow after *Me* and *My* will for your life, and *I* will grant the desires of your heart. This, *My* people, is the desire of your *Heavenly Father* that *My* people would choose to study *My* Holy Scriptures. Read them for they are food for your soul. Devour it!

MARCH 19, 2016

To Christians everywhere, now is not the time to sit back and be comfortable. The enemy is attacking *My* people in full force seeking whom he can devour. Christians pray for all nations and all its inhabitants. Intercede on their behalf, pleading the blood of the *Lamb* over all, especially family and friends. Pray for those in authority that they will seek *Me* and *My* guidance in all they do involving their fellow man. Most in authority make decisions that benefit them and their careers, not considering others around them. All people holding office or seeking an office should be aware of the decisions they make and how it will affect all mankind. Is there one among the people who cares for all humanity? There's more and more evil rising up now than ever in times before. *My* people, it's up to you to take charge and determine what's good and what's evil. The enemy has been defeated; Christians, take charge and don't let the enemy gain any more ground. You are the chosen generation. You possess the righteousness of *God*. Don't falter or log behind. You, *My* people, are the head not the tail. Don't accept anything less of anyone. Be aware of all promises made by individuals, promises they can't keep. Only by the hand of *God* can anyone rule or rein! By seeking *Me* in prayer, *I* will lead and guide all in positions of authority.

MARCH 21, 2016

My children, it's *My* strong desire for all *My* chosen ones to decree a day of rest, beginning with all social activities and all other engagements for one whole day that is set aside just for a day of rest and relaxation. *I*, the *God* and *Creator* of the universe, rested on the seventh day. You, *My* children, need to declare this also. Rest your body, soul, and spirit. Renewing comes from rest and relaxation. Sit back and enjoy a peaceful day. Let your thoughts be of *Me* and count your many blessings. *I* have poured out many blessings upon *My* children, but they were too busy to see them. That's why it's important to set aside a day of rest. Your mind and body need to rest from the activities to which you participate. Your mind needs to be refreshed in *Me*. This way, you can get a better perspective on making decisions. Step outside, if possible, and look all around. Whether it is in the city or the country, behold all *My* creations. These are all blessing from your *Heavenly Father*. Be grateful for all things and thankful for many things. Count your blessings! Be more observant of the people around you. Be a blessing to them. Look for the good in all people. There are still good Samaritans in your world. Rest and relaxation can lead to many new viewpoints on life. Enjoy *My* rest!

To all whom are lost, *My* patience grows short. The greatest miracle in the world, though lasting, it will not be everlasting. *I* am waiting for those who will finally make the decision to follow after *Me*. It's *My* desire that all *My* creations would accept *My* plan of salvation for all to spend eternity with *Me* and *My* kingdom. Yet many think they can continue in sin with no repentance or repercussions. There is a price to pay for all sins, one way or another. Sometimes the price may be death. Sometimes upon the approaching of death, they can receive forgiveness and accept *Me* that guarantees their place in *Heaven*. I'm waiting for all to come! The sin in the world is rapid, growing more evil daily. Instead of getting better, it constantly gets worse. The only hope for the lost is a *Savior*. If the lost could only see what *I* see, what's happening to all mankind. *I* see their torment, their thirst for violence, their hatred for their fellow men. Lost people of the world, can you not see all the violence committed to others? If you are tired of all this evil and seek an alternative, you will become one of *Mine* whom one day will rule and reign with *Me*. To all the lost, *I* say come. *My* patience is growing thin!

MARCH 23, 2016

To all *My* sons and daughters, are you prepared for the return of your *Lord and Savior*? Are you watching and listening for the trumpet call? Will you be caught off guard, or will you be on the alert and be ready for *My* coming? *My* children, once you have made the decision to follow after *Me*, you become *My* followers. You should always be on the alert and always watchful. Watching the signs of the times is important. You don't want to be caught off guard and left behind. The signs of the times are ever increasingly evil. When the people of your world took *Me* and *My* name out of everything, that's when they started seeing all the evil and violence. With *My* name and all the prayers of saints in public places, it provided a covering for your nation. Those in authority decided to take prayer from public places because it offended someone. They forgot about offending *God* Almighty who created all living things. It seems that man's opinions and rights are more important than the will of *God*! Now innocent people will suffer the consequences for those individuals. So be careful in whom you trust to make decisions for you. Seek *Me* above all else and leave the decision making in *My* capable hands. By the prayers of all the saints will the choice be made for your land.

*M*y brethren, it's *My* heart's desire that none of the lost should perish! *I* am waiting patiently for all *My* creations to find their way into *My* kingdom through repentance. It's *My* strong desire that all will seek *My* plan of salvation. In the end of times, *My* wrath will be poured out on all mankind to those that have refused to accept *My* salvation. Some people even don't believe yet in anything. Their minds become clouded and overcome by the enemy, and they don't know which way to turn. *I* sent *My* only begotten *Son* to your world to save the lost, yet they still don't believe. *He* was sent to free all captives from their strongholds. Still people turn away from *Him*. *He* stands with outstretched arms for all mankind to accept *His* love, grace, and compassion. Will you accept *Him*? Come, lost souls, and behold the *King* of kings! Come and see what's in store for those who accept *Him* and *His* kingdom. Come and see what is good!

MARCH 25, 2016

*M*y people, you own one of the most precious books in the world—your Holy Bible. It contains within its pages how the world and man came into existence. It contains the progress of mankind through the ages. Your Holy Bible tells of beautiful love stories, of battles, wars, and wonders beyond your imagination. It speaks of leaders and kings, good and bad. There contained in the Holy Scriptures are prophets and their prophetic sayings. The Holy Bible speaks about the bravery of men and women. Contained within the Holy Scriptures are the sacrifices of many for their faith. Great will be their reward. Inside the written *Word*, it speaks of the birth of *My* beloved *Son*. It shows *His* teachings and miracles while *He* walked upon the earth. Then read about *His* rejection and crucifixion. You can experience *His* love and grace. There are letters from *His* disciples that traveled with *Him*. There are letters to churches. The words are also to help *My* people live in their world. Abide by these sayings since they are inspired by the *Spirit of God*. Also contained in the Holy Bible are prophecies of things to come and how *My* people can avoid coming disasters. You see, you possess the most precious book given to all mankind. Cherish it and read it daily so you won't be misled by imposters. By knowing *My Word*, you are equipped to do battle with the enemy. Use *the Word of God* and the blood of *Jesus* against the devil. *His* time is limited. You see, *I* know the end of the story. *My* people guard against all negativity and evil-speaking people. You, *My* people, are a chosen generation. Hold your heads high and declare you belong to the *Most High*. Declare it daily and believe it. You are a chosen people, *My* people!

MARCH 26, 2016

People, people, people, those whom have ears, let them hear what *the Word of God* is saying to all who will listen. One day, every knee will bow, and every tongue will confess that *I* am *God*, the *Creator* of the universe. One day, all mankind will stand before *Me* in judgement. *My* people, are you ready to be judged by *God* Almighty? Have you lived your life in accordance with *My Word?* One day, you will be held accountable for every *Word* that proceeds from your mouth and every deed you've done in *My* name. Examine your way of life and see if it is according to *My* will. Seek *My* plans for your life. Seek *Me* in all things, and one day when you come before *Me*, *I* will say, "Well done, good and faithful servant. Enter in!"

MARCH 28, 2016

To all mankind, what do you not understand? That you are living in the last days and that the coming of the *Lord* is very soon, whether you are believers or idolaters! The people of your world are sitting back and allowing evil to overtake the innocent ones and do nothing. These actions and evil deeds should and will be punished. *My* people need to be prayed up and be on the alert, watching and listening for the trumpet call. If more people would look to *Me* for an answer to their woes and less to the world, things will begin to happen. Mankind is so wrapped up in the worldly matters; they forget who created the world. Seek ye the *Creator* of the world, not things of the world or people of the world. *I* say, *My* people, you need to be fasting and praying continually until you get a breakthrough. All Christians are being attacked around the world. *My* people be in prayer for all the innocent lives lost by terrorism attacks and all acts of violence. *I* say again, "Be on alert and on constant vigil. Remember, *I* am the great comforter and friend. Come to *Me* with all your cares, and *I* will no way turn you away. Seek *Me* above all else. *I* am the great *I Am!*"

To the bride of Christ, *I* am coming for a bride without spot or wrinkle. Are you *My* bride cleansed by the blood of the *Lamb*? Are your wedding garments white as snow, or are they stained with the things of the world? You, *My* bride, should be on the alert and prepared for your groom. Make every provision for *My* return. Be watchful about all the enemies' temptations. Be in constant prayer for your fellow man. Choose to form a closer relationship with your *Lord and Savior*. Rely on *Me* for all things, not the people of the earth. Do not follow after false teachings of those who claim to know the Scriptures. You can know *My Holy Word* forward and backward and yet not know *Me*. *My* people, to know *Me* is to sit quietly in *My Presence* and wait upon your *Lord*. Sing psalms to *Me* in worship. Prayer is essential in communing with your *Lord*. *My* bride, prepare yourself and make ready. Get your lives in order. You came into this world with nothing, and you will leave it with nothing; but oh, what a glorious day when you meet your groom face to face to spend eternity with *Me* in *My* kingdom. *I* will be back sooner than everyone thinks. Take heed and be watchful.

To all *My* people, how long? Oh! How long must *I* wait for you, *My* bride, to get your garments prepared? You, *My* people, are so wrapped up in the things of the world; you don't have the time for your *Bridegroom*. In your world when preparing for your wedding day, you make all the necessary preparations. *My* people, you should also prepare for your *Heavenly Groom*. Prepare for your heavenly wedding by getting to know your *Bridegroom*. This is accomplished by spending time in *My Holy Word*. Then *My* bride takes the time to come and sit beside *Me* and enter into *My Presence*. Talk and share with *Me* and then be still and listen your heart what your *Lord God* is speaking to you in that small voice. We can fellowship together. Then and only then can you get to know your *Bridegroom*, *My* bride (the church) should be watchful and alert. Seek ye first the kingdom of *God* and stay in communion with *Me* 24/7. *I* am just a thought and a prayer away. *My* people, *I* cannot impose enough how important it is for you to be ready to meet your *Bridegroom* in the blink of an eye. That's how fast death can come upon you. So it's imperative for all *My* people to be ready to meet *Me* and celebrate the great wedding supper of the *Lamb*.

APRIL 1, 2016

To all Christians, you possess all the power on earth when you use the name *Jesus*. This power has been given to you so you can come against and defeat the enemy, Satan. *My* people, you are sitting back and letting him gain a foothold into your lives. *He* is very sly and deceiving. Before you realize it, the enemy has entered in and promoted bad situations. *My* children, use the *God*-kind power to battle the father of all lies. Put on your full armor daily. Use the name *Jesus* frequently and declare in *Jesus* name the battle has already been won. If you are tired of all the bad and evil things, then do something about it. Don't just sit on your laurels and think about it. Be a doer of *the Word*! Say, "This far and no further devil. Stop in the name of *Jesus*. We are not going to take it anymore. You will cease as of right now."

APRIL 2, 2016

Chosen generation, in your houses of worship, you, *My* people, should set an example for others to follow by being humble in speech and appearance. Yet you need to be bold in the spirit when fighting with the enemy. You need not dress as the world does. Their belief is *less is more*. Not so, *My* children, be modest in your apparel, dressing for your *Lord and Savior*. Your desire is to please *Me* and no other. In your houses of worship, you are there to worship *Me* and spend time with *Me* and *My* chosen ones. You are not there to impress anyone. *My* children, *I* know your thoughts and your hearts. Come and be set apart from what the world has to offer. You live in the world, but you're not of the world. Take heed, *My* brethren, and show respect in your houses of worship as befitting children of the *Most High God*. Your method of dressing should in no way hinder the worship of your *Lord*. Let it be known that all of *God's* children show respect to all mankind and to love your neighbor as yourself.

APRIL 4, 2016

You, *My* children, are the branches of the one and only true vine, your *Lord and Savior*. As *My* branches reach out for sunlight, *I* want *My* branches (my children) to reach out to the lost souls and bring them into the light of your *Savior Jesus Christ*. Go seek *My* children for all who are going nowhere fast. Show them how to slow down their pace and enjoy the peace of the vine, which is the *Creator*. The lost are travelling so fast; they don't know how go at a slower pace. You, *My* children, are the light in this darkened world. It's up to you to seek all who are oppressed, addicted, lowly of spirit, unloved, unwanted, the most undesirable and show them the love of your *Heavenly Father*. Most lost ones of the world have been thrown out like yesterday's trash. *I* am the great trash collector, and I'm waiting for all to come. *I* will deliver them of their affliction and show them the love like they have never known. Go and bring all the lost into *My* kingdom!

APRIL 5, 2016

People of the world, once *I* stepped down from *Heaven* and into your darkened world, *I* came into your world to show the way to *Heaven*. Beckoning all to partake of *My* salvation, *I* bring the glorious light to the world. No one comes to the *Father* except through *Me*. *I* came down to the earth *I* created expecting more Christians. Instead, *I* was met with rejection, deceit, denial, and punishment. *I* just wanted the people to see the love of *My Father* by the works and miracles *I* did. *I* was only doing the will of *My Father*. Some understood; others scoffed and ridiculed *My* teachings. Some were true followers of the faith and continued with *My* teachings and sharing it with others. When people don't understand something, they dismiss it as wrong. The prophets of old predicted the coming of the messiah coming to earth and walking among the people and performing many miracles, and yet only a few believed. In this darkened and sinful world, the only hope for all mankind is *Jesus Christ* the light of the world.

APRIL 6, 2016

*M*y children, why can't you realize the intensity of the love that *I* have for *My* children? Sometimes it's difficult for *My* people to accept or understand the fullness of *My* love for them. Some may see *Me* as the *Father* that punishes when *My* children fall into sin. As with earthly parents, when your children do wrong, they are corrected. *I* as your *Heavenly Father* correct all those *I* love, some more so than others. *My* ways of correction may be more of guidance along the pathway of life. *My* love is unconditional, and you cannot earn it by anything you do. Only by accepting *My* plan of salvation is it accomplished. Just accept the love *I've* freely given to all those who will acknowledge *Me* as their *Lord and Savior*. You see, *My* children, this is real love from a *Father*!

APRIL 6, 2016 P.M.

People, you possess the power which was given to *Jesus*. You can conquer all the giants in your life. You are equipped with everything you need. It's a matter of how you use this power. Be bold and stand firm without giving in or giving up. It's *My* desire for the nations of the world to stand up for their faith and convictions. The nations of the world have become complacent and lazy in their faith, relying on others to do the work in which they were called! Christians of the world, when will you assume the power and authority that has been given to you by *God Almighty*? It's been freely given for your benefit. It won't do you any good if you don't use it. It's available now for those who will use it.

Don't delay; start immediately using the *God*-given power that has been bestowed on you. Act upon it; declare it in the name of the *Lord*.

APRIL 7, 2016

To all *My* followers, as *I* look about the land of *My* followers, they look the same as all the lost of the world. *My* people should have the joy of the *Lord*, expressing it by their countenance. Christians walk around with gloom and doom on their faces. They should all understand that greater is *He* that is in them than *He* that's in the world. Let the joy and presence of your *Heavenly Father* glow all about you. Let the presence of the *Lord* rise up within you and then demonstrate the love and joy of the *Lord*. *I* come to your world to set the captives free from sin and to show the love of the *Father*. That should make *My* followers elated, yet looking upon their faces, you would never know they had been set free. Sometimes people become burdened with the problems of daily life. They forget who gave them life. Bring all your burdens to *Me*, and *I* will give you joy and peace unspeakable. *My* people should be the happiest people on earth because they will soon spend eternity with *Me*. That's enough to shout about and make joyful noises unto the *Lord*.

APRIL 8, 2016

Born-again believers, who do you say that *I* am? To some who is facing problem after problem, *I* am wonderful counselor. To others, *I* can move the mountains in their life. So *I* am *Mighty God*. Yet some needing love and forgiveness, *I* am everlasting *Father*. Still to others in this upside-down world, *I* am the Prince of peace. Now, believers, whom do you say that *I* am? When you receive *My* plan of salvation, *I* became all these to you. *I* am your everything! Rest in the knowledge that *I* am whatever you need. Just call upon *My* name, and *I* will in no way cast your side. *I* am your next breath, your next heartbeat. Rely on *Me* for all your needs. All you have to do is call out to *Me* in your hour of difficult times. Just cry out and say *Jesus*. *I* encourage all believers to rely on *Me* more and less on their own abilities. You can do nothing on your own, only with Christ who strengthens you. *That's who I am!*

All *My* children, it's the desire of your *Father's* heart to have an up-close and personal relationships with all *My* followers. Everything in your world has become so impersonal. Everyone has turned to electronics for conversation instead of the personal touch of talking one-on-one. The people of your world are starving for love, affection, companionships, even someone to converse with. The sounds of the human voice have been replaced with electronic gadgets. *My* children, think about the people who don't own or can't use the electronic devices, mostly the elderly. It's your place as *My* children to reach out to those that are unreachable with your electronics. Pick up the telephone and call someone. It's time for people to go back to basics, reach out to someone even just to say hello. Let it be known that *My* children are of the chosen generation that cares for all people. Reach beyond your inner circle and develop relationships with all your brothers and sisters in Christ. Take notice especially of the older people and spend some quality time with them. Be a blessing to others with a human touch of kindness.

APRIL 10, 2016

All the followers of the *Lord Jesus Christ*, be ye doers of *the Word of God* and not hearers only. Even the enemy can quote scriptures. So if *My* followers aren't acting upon *My Word*, then they must be sitting back and watching others use it. *My Word* is to be put to use every day, not just for your convenience. It's food for the soul. Feed upon it daily for your spiritual nourishment. Contained in *My* Holy Scriptures are the plans for your life. They tell you how to defeat the enemy, how to become a better person, how to increase your finances, and most of all, how to live in this world of sin. Be reading and studying *My Word* daily; you can be prepared for all the fiery darts the enemy will throw at you. In *the Word*, you are told how to do battle by putting on the full armor of *God*. Henceforth you will be protected. Don't misuse or change *My Words*! Study and research for their meaning and how they can be applied to your daily life. Be doers of *the Word* by going out into your world and declaring what *the Word of God* is saying to all people.

APRIL 12, 2016

*M*y chosen generation! You are being watched and continually condemned by all the people of your world. They believe that all Christians are hypocrites, saying and professing one thing and doing something different, changing with the times and not standing on their faith. It's easy to declare something, but when some Christians are put to the test, they change directions and beliefs like the wind. *My* people, you need to be firm in your beliefs and be careful in your dealings with nonbelievers. Watch your choice of words. Let them be compassionate and uplifting, full of love and concern. Do not judge others by their demeanor or dress and appearance. Sometimes people will confront you, appearing immoral just to see your reaction. In speaking with these individuals in your mind (thought life), be silently praying for them. Sometimes the lost don't want you praying for them where others might see. The lost are so self-conscious of what others will think when they become one of *My* chosen ones.

APRIL 13, 2016

Followers of the *Lord Jesus Christ*, why concern yourselves about tomorrow and your future? *I* hold tomorrow and your future in *My* hands. *My* people, do not be concerned about food or clothing. *I* will take care of all your needs. *I* am your provider and know of your needs even before you ask *Me* for them. *I* am the all-knowing *God*. You, *My* people, just concern yourselves with doing the will of your *Heavenly Father*. *I* will take care of your needs and desires. *I* don't want *My* followers to worry about anything. Worry is a sin; it means that you can't or don't trust *Me* to do what *I* say *I* will do. *My Word* is true, and *I* cannot lie. *I* will receive *My* own and will supply all their needs according to *My* riches in *Heaven*. It's up to *My* followers to believe *My Word* and the promises I've made. They need to lean not on their own understanding but by faith believe in *Me*. *My* followers, put all your faith and trust in your *Lord and Savior*. Make your entire request known and believe that *I* will answer them!

APRIL 14, 2016

*M*y people, you have heard the Scripture which says, "Judge not, lest you be judged by the same manner you judge others." *I* say to you, "Do not judge others by the standards of the world but by *God's* word." There are several different standards whereby we are to look at others. You should use godly wisdom and moral courage together with *God's* written word to distinguish between right and wrong. You cannot make judgments on others if you are committing the same sin. Do not sound like a know-it-all nor that you are superior to others. This is not the way to correct someone. In confronting others living in sin, do this with the love and compassion of the *Lord*. Speak softly; do what you think is right. You can only let the *Holy Spirit* lead and guide you with the proper words to say, and then let *God* do the rest. When talking or discussing morality to others, let it be known that there is a *Savior* that forgives all sin, but first, the people must seek *Him*!

*M*y chosen generation, the world you live in is trying to dictate what you, *My* people, can say or do regarding your faith. While yet living in this world of yours, you must abide by man's rules unless they go against *the Holy Word of God*. Stand firm in *My Holy Word* because *My Word* must come first. So then and only then when man's rules or laws go against *God's Holy Word* do you disobey the laws of the lands. You as *My* chosen generation are to read and study *My Word* daily so that you will know what *I* am saying to *My* people. *My* Holy Scriptures are for you to live by and to be guided in your life by them. Use *the Word of God* in making all decisions. Those people whom call themselves Christians and yet do opposite of what *the Word of God* says, *I* say are hypocrites. *My* people, take every thought captive and don't believe everything you hear. Believe only in *the Word of God*. When people's words don't line up with *the Word*, then disregard them. Only believe if the words are partnered with the Bible. People are so known by the fruits they bear! Watch and pray!

APRIL 16, 2016

Christians, do you understand what it means to take up your cross and follow after *Me*? It means that there is no one more important than *I* and the plans *I* have for you. It means your family will laugh and mock you because of your belief. You will lose friends and family members. People you thought were your friends will suddenly find excuses to stay away or not talk to you at all. To take up your cross and follow after *Me* means you will suffer trials and tribulations. *I* also suffered at the hands of *My* people. Those who endure until the end and don't waver, great is their reward. So look up, *My* followers, and be watchful for the coming of the *Lord* draws even closer than people think. Be prepared, *My* people. Stay in close relationship with *Me* and reap the benefits.

*M*y children, *I* speak, and you do not listen. You have ears, and yet you do not hear what the *Spirit of the Lord* is saying to *His* people. You have eyes, and yet you don't see *Me* working in your lives. Take up your cross and follow after *Me*. Forget about all else and seek after the things of *My* kingdom. Take up your sword daily by putting on the full armor of *God*. Speak to your infirmities, your illness, your pain and suffering, the sickness of mind, soul, and spirit. Speak healing in all these areas. Follow with belief and keep believing and trusting until the healing has manifested in the natural. *My* children, these are battles all around you. Be in constant prayer regarding all these battles and situations. You are more than a conqueror, so declare *the Word of the Lord* and the blood of the *Lamb* over all. Remember, the battle has already been won; the enemy has been defeated!

APRIL 18, 2016

*M*y people, why are you letting the powers of evil reign in your world? You, *My* children, need to take charge and demand to be free, free from all chains that bind you, freedom that was said for many years ago. When will *My* people use the power given to them? The same power that *Jesus* possesses. *My* people, you've been called out of darkness into *My* marvelous light. You've been given great power, and yet it's not being used. Why are you allowing the sins of the world to get into your homes, your lives, marriages, finances, and the lives of your family members? How long will you be a part of what's going on in your society? *My* heart aches because *My* people have been conformed to this world, and most are afraid to speak out. People are being sacrificed continually. Bond together in prayer for all who are persecuted and tortured. Believers use the authority that has been passed on to you. Use the name of *Jesus*.

*M*y brothers and sisters, are you going about doing the will of our *Heavenly Father*? Are you proclaiming *the Word of God* to all who will listen? Are you telling others of *His* marvelous works and *His* many blessings? Have you spoken of the end of times and the second coming of the *Son of God*? Speak of all the attributes of your *Heavenly Father*. Tell others of *His* power to forgive and the love *He* has for all mankind. Explain how *He* is always willing to listen to the requests of *His* children, how *He* longs for *His* children to come into *His* presence and worship him. *He* longs for *His* creations to learn more about *Him* and *His* kingdom. *My* brothers and sisters, you all belong to *God the Father*. You have been grafted into the family of *God*. Proclaim how your *Father* loved *His* creations so much that *He* sent *His* only begotten *Son* to die for them so they could share in the kingdom of *God*. Go out unto the lost, *My* brothers and sisters, and tell them about your *Heavenly Father* and the love *He* has for all.

Friends, do you consider yourselves a friend of the *Almighty God*? Do you come daily and discuss all your problems, care, and concerns with *Me*? If you truly are *My* friend, then why haven't you let go and let *God* handle all your situations? *I* am here waiting for you to enter into *My* throne room. There are so many people in today's world requiring desperately a true friend to converse with. *I* am the true friend. Yet they still run to and fro looking in all the wrong directions. Look up, people! *I* am here omnipresent waiting for someone to call out *My* name. Just call out *My* name, and *I* will hear you, and if you are one of the lost and will accept *My* plan of salvation, *I* will be your *Father*, friend, comforter, and everything to you. *I* am the great *I Am*. Friends of *Mine*, upon accepting salvation, rejoice in the knowledge that you have been joined with *Me* in *Heaven*. Then you will be called *My* friend!

APRIL 21, 2016

My people, you the followers of the *Lord Jesus Christ* are the redeemed, the righteousness of *God*, forgiven, sanctified, and purchased for a price! You have been given the same power and authority as *Jesus*. Yet you, *My* people, are reluctant to use it. *I* say, why do you sit quietly and let the enemy walk all over you? Are you concerned about others and what they will say when you start taking authority over the enemy? Don't be afraid to use the *God*-given power over the evils of the world. Being fearful is not an acceptable word. Step out of your comfort zone. Be bold for the *God* of the universe is with you, in you, and all around you. Go forth and lay hands on the sick believing what you pray for will manifest in the natural. Seek the kingdom of *God* first and foremost, and all these things will be given unto you. It seems that *My* people can't fathom or understand the real power they possess. All they have to do is believe, and it will be so! Comprehend what *I* am saying, and let it penetrate into your spirit. Then as Lazarus came forth from the tomb, let *My* people awaken from a long sleep they have been in for some time. It's time for them to go out into the nations and proclaim *the Word of the Lord* and *His* salvation for all mankind. Use your *God*-given power and pray for all *My* creations that they will seek *My* plan of salvation and the kingdom of *God*!

APRIL 22, 2016

*M*y brethren, *I* want that you should take an examination today. We are going to examine your heart and the words that are verbally spoken. Remember, what you speak comes from the heart. Have you spoken harshly of another individual? Maybe you said something about them or against them. If this is true, then you need to seek forgiveness and be more watchful of what you say. The words coming out of your mouth should edify people, not dishonor or discredit them or even speak harshly about them. Stop and examine the thoughts and words you speak. Take a look down deep in your heart and spirit to see if there are things that can defile you. If so, seek *Me*, and *I* will create in you a clean heart made of flesh, not stone. Sometimes, *My* brethren, by the evil things you see can enter into your heart without you realizing it. Next thing you notice are some bad thoughts you have against another. Examine your hearts daily to see if there be any evil in them that can defile you.

APRIL 23, 2016

Come, all the people of world who profess that they are Christ followers or Christians. Come before *Me* and seek *My* face. Everything you have need of is found in *My* kingdom. Come all you who are burdened with problems of the world laid upon your shoulders. Bring all problems to *Me*, and *I* will give you rest. Come all who have been rejected and cast out. *I* will in no way cast you aside but will give you love and compassion. Come to those who are depressed, and *I* will give you joy unspeakable. Come all who are sick in mind and body. *I* will heal thee. *I* took stripes on *My* back for your healing. Come to those whom are needy. *I* will supply all your needs according to the riches in *Heaven*. Come to those who lack courage, and *I* will give you boldness. Come those who lack in finances. Give and it will be given back unto you ten and hundredfold. Come with your prayers for other nations in distress. *I* am in their midst, yet they do not see. When you come into *My Presence*, *I* mean for you to bring all your problems, sickness, disease, cares, and woes to *Me*, and *I* will give you rest. What *I* am saying to all *My* people—come unto *Me*!

APRIL 25, 2016

*M*y people, in this life once you have chosen to follow *Me*, you will be subjected to many things. You will lose a lot of your rights as a Christian. People of influence will laugh and scoff at your beliefs saying they are out of context with the world. They don't realize that believing godly people was how your nation was founded. It was started with godly principles. These were *God*-fearing men. They put *God* in every aspect of their decision-making. They were not ashamed to speak the name of the *God*, nor were they too proud to give *God* the credit for help in time of need. They believed in *God* and abided by godly virtues. They also were persecuted, but most did not back down. In today's world, you can't even speak the name of *God* or *Jesus* in public without retributions. Pastors of churches are threatened daily for their beliefs. Some are even put in jail or prison. Behold, great is the reward for those who are true and faithful and hold on until the end!

*M*y child, do not question the gifts *I* have given to you. Use them for the glory of your *Heavenly Father*. You are like an open vessel, and *I'm* pouring *My Spirit* into you so as to fill you up. Use your gifts wisely. They are not for show but to edify the kingdom of *God*. You, *My* child, have made yourself and your spouse available to *Me* to be used in *My* plans of salvation. Go out into this evil world and declare the king is coming. *He* is coming very soon! Tell *My* people to listen to what the *Spirit of God* is saying and to be prepared for the coming of the *Lord*. Tell them to examine their hearts carefully. Any unknown or known sin, seek forgiveness. Tell *My* people to prepare for their *King*. One day in the blink of an eye, the trumpet will sound, and all the dead in Christ will rise first then *My* saints will come to meet *Me* in the sky. Examine yourselves so as not to be left behind when the trumpet sounds!

*M*y chosen generation, do you desire wisdom and or knowledge? Seek *Me*, and *I* will fill you up to overflowing. Do you have a need? *I* am the great provider! Whatever your request, *I* am the one to seek. Do you want to commune with *Me*? Read the Holy Scriptures and begin to converse with *Me* in prayer. By reading and studying the written *Word of God*, you will be able to understand *My* plans for all mankind. You, *My* chosen ones, can see all the promises and blessings that *I* have bestowed on you *My* people. Take notice, Christians, a roaring lion going to and fro seeking whom *He* can devour. You have your weapons of warfare, *My Holy Word*; use it! Don't just carry it with you to your church service; use it daily. Study and read it daily. There are people quoting *My Word* constantly out of context. They use the Scriptures to their own advantage. That's not how *My* words were meant to be used. They are to benefit, lead, and guide *My* followers through their pathway of life.

APRIL 28, 2016

For all the Christian people from every nation and tongue, from all generations, *I* say *come*! Come to the one who forgives all your sins, past, present, and future; one who knows all your thoughts, all your desires, and all your dreams. *I* even know the number of hairs on your head. *I* know every heartbeat and every breath you take because you were created in *My* image. To all people around the world who belong to the kingdom of *God*, *I* say you are precious in *My* sight. You are the righteousness of *Jesus Christ*. You are *My* beloved in whom holds the power and authority that was given to *Jesus*. Now *I* say, assert yourselves and make it known that you are a Christian and follow the teachings of the *Lord Jesus Christ* because *His* teachings will lead and guide you through this life, and by *His* promises, you will spend the next life in eternity with him. People everywhere, if you have chosen to follow after *Me*, then make your declaration and say, "I love *the Word of God*. It directs my life. It gives me the promises of *God* if I follow it." Stand up, *My* people, and be counted among all believers around the world. *My* people, let *Me* see boldness, not meekness; standing firm, not weakness or backing down or giving in.

Christians, *I* asked a question years ago of *My* disciples: Whom do you say that *I* am? Now as *My* followers, can you tell others who *I* am? If so, then are you planting seeds of *the Word* all around and about you? It seems that some are so involved with the things of the world; you forget who is first and foremost in your life. *My* people should not be afraid to say that they are Christians and to speak up for *the Word of God*. You are the righteousness of Christ. You became a new creation when you accepted the plan of salvation, and old things have passed away. You will begin to see things in a different light. You will behold all people with a different attitude and outlook. Eventually you will see others as *I* see them with love for all. You should treat others as you want to be treated. You should pray daily and read the Scriptures daily. Be thankful for all things and proclaim the blessings of the *Lord*! That's who you are!

APRIL 30, 2016

Believers, as you are traveling in your pathway of life, you will encounter all types of individuals. Some will profess that they are followers of *Jesus*. Yet when tried and tested become like the Pharisees and Sadducees. Some are for show with their great speeches and great knowledge of *the Word*. While others put on their happy face for all to see that they are followers of Christ, yet behind closed doors, there is a different attitude regarding their beliefs. *My people*, do not do as the hypocrites; stay true to *the Word of God*. Do not waver, being one way one day and another way the day after. Stay true to yourselves and to your *Lord and Savior* who does not change according to the situation. *I* never change. *I* am the same yesterday, today, and forever. *I* expect *My* believers to be the same way. Circumstances should not change your opinions one iota. Stay true to *Me* as *I* am true to you!

MAY 3, 2016

A chosen generation, in this life and in this wicked world, there may come a time when you will be put to a test regarding your faith. You, *My* people, will be asked to acknowledge *Me* or deny knowing *Me*. When that time comes or if and when it comes, be prepared to face the consequences by declaring you are a follower of the *Lord Jesus Christ*. *My* name in your world today is not permitted to be spoken. Yet there are true believers when tested will not back down. If the people in your land would turn from their wicked ways and repent, *I* would heal their land. Getting individuals to understand and believe is an entirely different conception. Some don't believe in a *Creator*; some don't believe in *Heaven* or hell. One day upon approaching death, they will find one place or another is their eternal destination, but you see then it's too late. If they don't accept *Me* before death, then their fate is set. *I* want all *My* people to spend eternity with *Me*. When you, *My* chosen generation, go out into your world and speak of an eternal kingdom, people look at you and wonder where you are coming from. They turn deaf ears to *the Words* of the *Lord*. Then when some catastrophe happens, they then begin to call out *My* name in desperation. *I* am always there for anyone seeking forgiveness and/or salvation.

MAY 4, 2016

My brethren, be ye not concerned with the ways of the world. Just be concerned about the things of *God*. You, *My* people, are blessed among all nations, and yet some of you complain. The ways of the world are trivial in comparison to the plans for all *My* brethren. It's up to them to seek *Me* and *My* plans for their life. Some will compare themselves and their lives to others. You, *My* children, are bought with a price. The others you envy are under the influence of the enemy. Seek *My* will, and blessings will follow. *I* will pour out the blessings of *Heaven* for all those who seek after *Me*. *I* am a loving *Father*. When *My* children ask for bread, *I* will not give them a stone. The same power that was given to *Jesus* has been given to you, *My* brethren. It's been placed inside of you to use. Many people don't understand this gift. It's there to be used by all *My* followers.

MAY 5, 2016

Christians, years ago, Moses asked Pharaoh to let his people go. It took many plagues upon the Pharaoh and his people before he would let the children of Israel go. Today, you see many plagues put on your nation and the world by the enemy. They are sickness, diseases, famine, fires, floods, and earthquakes. By keeping *My* people so involved and concerned with all this, they don't take the time to spend with the *Lord*. This is how *He* keeps people in bondage. It's up to all Christians to declare to the enemy that *He* was defeated on the cross and has no claim on *God's* property. Christians, you are in a battle of the mind, body, and spirit. Take the authority *I* have given unto you and use it to break the chains of darkness. Many of *My* people are not equipped to do battle, yet you have been given the same power a *Jesus* when *He* rose from the grave. Some are too meek and shy and rely on others to defeat the enemy. You cannot defeat any enemy with meekness. You have to be bold and seek *My* strength. Remember, nothing is impossible for *Me*. Together we can break the ties that bind. *I* will lead you out of bondage, just as *I* brought *My* people from Egypt. Come, *My* children, and *I* will in no way reject you!

MAY 6, 2016

In *My* quiet time with the *Lord*, *I* asked *Him* what *He* would have *Me* say to *His* people. *I* say to those who have ears, let them hear what *the Word of God* is saying. *My* people, *I* stepped down into your world to bring life everlasting. *I* came so that people would be free from all the ties that bind. Yet *My* people are still running to and fro, asking where you are, *Lord*. *My* people, *I* am here all around you, in front, behind, beside, and indwelling in you. Just take the time and listen to *My* voice and behold all the marvelous wonders awaiting you. There will be times of trials and tribulations. Be of good cheer. *I* have overcome the world. In times of trials, lean on *Me*, and *I* will comfort and deliver you. *I* know what you have need of before you ask. *I* just want *My* people to learn to depend on *Me* more and more until *I* become your first thought upon awakening and your last thought before retiring to bed. Remember, *My* people, I've loved you enough that *I* laid *My* life down for you so you and *I* can spend eternity together. It's up to you to develop the closeness with *Me*. *I* will not push or prod you. *I* want *My* people to come willingly.

My chosen ones, *I* want to be your everything. Every need you have, *I* can provide; just come to *Me* and make your requests known. You see, *I* know your needs before you even ask for them, yet *I* wait patiently for you *My* chosen ones to take the time and seek *Me* for all your needs. *I* can supply all that you have need of in accordance with *My Word*. The reason *I* want *My* chosen ones to come to *Me* for all their heart desires—you see, *My* chosen ones, *I* desire for you, *My* people, to spend time with *Me* and in *My Presence*. By coming before *Me* making their request known, they are committed to spending a few moments with *Me*, the *Heavenly Father*. *I* have need of all *My* chosen ones to come before *Me* in worship and prayer. Seek *My* ways and seek after the heavenly things, and *I* will supply your earthly desires. All *I* want and need from *My* children is to put *Me* above everything in your life. Keep your thoughts, prayers, and worship of *Me* only!

MAY 9, 2016

People of faith, seasons may come, and seasons may go. People may come into your life for a season, and then they are gone. Things that's happening in your world are temporary! Your lives are only temporary. Everything you see all around you is just for a while, temporary. Seasons change; your lives change. One thing that does not change is *the Word of God*. It is forever true and faithful. *I, God Almighty*, do not change. *I* am the same yesterday, today, and forever. No exceptions! Take heed, believers, and know that you can count on *the Word of God* to be true in all circumstances. What was spoken years ago can be interpreted for use in your everyday life. It's easily accessible and free to all who partake. It will heal you; it will comfort and console you, and it will bind all the chains of the enemy. It's full of information to guide you in your daily living. It never changes, although sometimes individuals interpret the meanings differently. Rely on *My* unchanging *Holy Spirit* to give you the right understandings for your needs. We, the *Father, Son,* and *Holy Spirit* never change. You have *My Word* on that!

MAY 10, 2016

Words of wisdom! A minute, an hour, a day, a week, a month, and a year, once they've come and gone, it can never be relived. So *I* say, be careful of every word that proceeds out of your mouth. The words you speak should edify people and encourage them. Don't utter useless words that can harm someone. Think a moment before speaking because once spoken, those words cannot be taken back. Every minute, think thoughts of your *Heavenly Father*. Every hour, give *Him* your praise. Every day, seek your *Father* and *His Holy Word* in prayer. Every week or more, visit your houses of worship. Once a month, visit the elderly either in a nursing facility or the ones that are home bound. Every year, be grateful for all the blessings of the previous year and look ahead for the blessings yet to come. When looking back at the past year, don't look at what you should have done but what you can do in the future to further the kingdom. Live the minutes, hours, and weeks to the glory of *God*. Decide on how you can reach the lost and bring them into the kingdom. Make every minute, hour, day, and week worthwhile because once the time has passed, it is gone forever. Use your time wisely because one day you will give an account of all your words! Be wise in all things pertaining to *God*.

My people, as your world seems to be spinning out of control, do not be dismayed, for *I* have overcome the world. *My* people need to rise up and take control of all the situation before them. Do not back up or back down from anything the devil throws at you. You are the redeemed and righteousness of *God*. Put on your armor, take up your position, and prepare for battle. In *My* strength, you can conquer the enemy. Declare, "We will not be defeated. We will not be overcome. We are children of the *Most High God* who has conquered the world." It may seem as though the enemy is gaining ground. *He* can only gain the ground that *My* people permit *Him* to claim. So you see, it's up to you to determine what you will let *Him* acquire. Say *stop* to everything *He* is doing or about to do. Tell *Him* you are a child of the living *God* and won't take it anymore. Start trampling *Him* under your feet. Start declaring that *He* has been defeated and no longer in control of anything in your life or the lives of all family members. Come against *Him* in regard to your nation and the world. Pray, pray, pray. That's the answer to all the problems affecting *My* people.

MAY 12, 2016

*M*y children, are there any sick among you? In your houses of worship, are there sick among you? If so, call the elders together to lay hands on them and pray for their healing. It's *My* will for all to be healed. It's by faith that you will be healed by believing in the *Lord God Almighty* that *He* will heal all those that are afflicted with diseases of the enemy. Some people are healed while others' healing is gradual. Unknown sin or unforgiveness can hinder healing. There are those who believe that they are supposed to suffer as *I* did. *I* suffered on the cross so *My* people wouldn't have to. The only things *My* followers will suffer are persecutions because of their faith. To say that *I* put sickness and diseases on *My* people is erroneous. When *I* walked among the people, *I* healed their diseases and cast out demons. *I* was not sick with cancer, diabetes, heart disease, etc., so it's *My* will for the people to be healed. The diseases are the enemy's plan to draw you away from the healer, to keep your mind set on the afflictions and not on the one who took stripes on *His* back for their healing!

MAY 14, 2016

People of faith, when are you going to be bold and take a stand for your faith? People, do not remain silent any longer; speak up and speak out! You, Christian people, are *My* voice delivering the words of the Holy Bible to all the nations. Don't stay silent any longer. Make your statements regarding your beliefs known to all mankind. Some are speaking out while others remain silent. No longer, *My* people, shall you remain silent and let others make choices for you. They will speak words from their heart and mind which is defiled with the things of the world. You speak by the spirit of the living *God* the things of *God*. *I* gave your hands to lay on the sick for healing, arms for hugging your brothers and sisters in *Christ* and showing the love of *God*, feet and legs for walking the distance to reach the lost, feet for stepping on the enemy. Put *Him* under your feet! You are in the latter days, *My* people, so be prayed up and stand up and be counted among Bible-believing Christians around the world. Don't accept man's laws when they go against *My Holy Word*. The *Holy Word of God* is for *My* followers to live by and to be led by it in their pathway of life. Speak up now and let all declare *the Word* of the living *God*.

MAY 16, 2016

My child, why do you think you need the words from an evangelist to tell you to keep on the path *I* have prepared for you? Open your ears and eyes to be one whom has set you on your road to victory. There will be many people you will come in contact with that will have words of wisdom. Heed their words and prayers for healing. Just remember that *I* am the true *God* in whom all revelations and power began. I've given the same power that was given to *My Son, Jesus,* to all believers that partake of *His* salvation. Likewise, all ministers, preachers, and evangelists have been given the same power too. So you, *My* child, get your messages and revelations from *Me,* the one and only true *God.* By being faithful in studying *My Word* and sitting in *My Presence* daily, you gain knowledge and spiritual blessings from *God* himself. Do not doubt your gifts; they are blessings for all who will partake and heed. *I* say good and faithful servant! This is what the *Spirit of the Lord* says.

MAY 17, 2016

Christians everywhere, the lost of the world are perishing from lack of knowledge. They are starving for nourishment for their bodies, love and compassion from someone who cares. Christians, you possess the answers to all their needs. It's a question of how to get you, *My* people, out of your comfort zone to go and witness of the blessings they have in store for all who come to *My* kingdom. Speak to them of being able to come to *Me* with any need which they may have in store for all who come to *My* kingdom. Explain to them upon their accepting *My* plan of salvation: *I* will supply all their needs according to *My* riches in glory. *I* will be their friend, healer, provider, and constant companion, their everything. Some have never heard *the Word of God* spoken, and some don't even know what *the Word of God* is. Christians, you have become complacent in your outlook about the lost. The harvest is ripe in your area. It's up to you as followers of the *Lord* to go out and seek all those who are lost and dying from lack of knowledge. It's in your hands; you decide. *I* have given you *My Word* to pass on to others. You have the power and the weapons of warfare, so go forth to all the nations!

People of faith, *I* welcome you into the holy of holies; come, *My* people, and experience the goodness of your *Heavenly Father*. Come into *My Presence* with worship, gratefulness, love, honor, and adoration for your *Father*. Come declaring your faithfulness, your servitude, and receive *My* blessings. Come, people of faith, from all the four corners of the earth into the heavenly realm. Come in spirit and worship the *God* of the universe. *I* am spirit; you must worship *Me* in spirit. You, people of faith, have been redeemed and can come before *Me* in spirit. Come into the throne room of your *God*. Come and exalt *Him* above all others. You are as welcome as *Jesus* is. Come, *I* say, come.

To *My* beloved children, as *My* children, you have been accepted into the kingdom of *God* with all privileges as *Jesus*. Come, *My* chosen ones, and rejoice for the kingdom of *God* is close at hand. *My* beloved, you are already experiencing persecutions, anger, disasters. People, these are signs mentioned in *My Holy Word*. Are you prepared for *My* second coming? Are you watchful, alert, and on guard? You must be forever on guard because *My* returning can happen at any moment. You will experience many things on a national level as well as local. Other faiths ridicule your belief in a living *God*. They don't believe in the resurrection or in the rapture of the saints. Trying to communicate about the true living *God* sometimes seems impossible, but with *God*, nothing is impossible. It takes *My* chosen ones to be in constant continual prayer for all nations around the world and for all the different faiths to come together as believers in the *Lord Jesus Christ*. You, *My* beloved children, are *My* messengers, ministers, and evangelist that *I* have chosen to bring forth *the Word of God* to all nations!

My friends, when *I* walked among the people years ago, *I* had many followers. Some were seeking after healings, some seeking deliverance from the attacks of the enemy. Yet there were those who were paralyzed and still others with deformities. *I* healed all that came before *Me*. *I* never turned any away. When it became time for *My* followers to depart, *I* fed them all. Everywhere *I* went, people followed seeking after *Me*. When *My* time came that *I* was to be betrayed and then falsely accused, where were the people that *I* had helped? Where were the followers? There was not one to speak in *My* defense. *I* stood alone to do *My Father's* will and fulfill the scriptures. In your world, you have friends. Are they true friends and will stand beside you no matter what happens? Will they be there when you call upon them? Can you count on them in your time of need? If so, then you could count them as true friends. True friends are always there when you need them. You see, *I* am your true friend when you accept *My* salvation. *I* will always be there for you. *I* never sleep nor slumber so you can rest in *Me* completely.

MAY 21, 2016

Christians around the world, make your declarations of faith known. Declare *the Word of the Lord*. Do not back down, nor do not be afraid or reluctant to speak. For *I* am with you now and always. Speak up, *My* people, about all the wrong things happening in your world. Speak out against all the wrong teachings that have been perpetrated against all Christians. If more of *My* followers would make their voices heard, then you would start to see things changing. The enemy is showing himself more because *My* people don't speak out. All your declarations of faith must line up with *the Word of God*. When speaking out about any situation, make sure it lines up with *My Word*. People can change words to suit themselves, which happens a lot of the time. *My Holy Word* does not change. It remains forever, no compromises; it's very explicit and says what is true. Christians read the Holy Scriptures daily so you will know what's true and what's false. By researching and reading the Scriptures, you will not be misled. *My* people should be knowledge-able of *the Word*. Not speaking up and keeping silent has allowed all the other voices to prevail. *My* people should stand up and be bold and not be overcome or overtaken. The enemy is taking territories that belong to *My* people. All because the Christians won't speak up and speak out. Heed *My* warning and make your voices heard among all nations.

MAY 23, 2016

Brothers and sisters in the *Lord*, you are the plants from seeds planted long ago by someone witnessing or preaching *the Word of God* to you. In order to grow from seedlings into plants, you must feed on the *Holy Word of God* for the food of the soul. This should be a daily requirement. You can't grow if you are not fed. Feeding in *the Word* increase your faith. The *Holy Word* will fill all aspects of your life. It is the only spiritual food you will ever need. It won't do you any good if you don't partake of it and all its promises and blessings. You will be like a seed that was just planted. If it's not watered, it will die. So as to the words that were spoken to you, if they are not watered or feed with *the Word of God* will wilt and die from lack of nourishment. *My* people, feed on *My* precious *Holy Word* morning, noon, and night. Partake of it because it will encourage you, bless you, and fill you up to overflowing. It brings healing, forgiveness, deliverance, and peace if you follow it. Seek *the Word of God*!

MAY 24, 2016

Children of the *Most High*, do you partake of the privilege sitting in the presence of the *Most High God*? Some of *My* children in today's world think it difficult to come and spend time in *My Presence*. It's easy, and yet so few have accepted *My* invitation. Some don't understand and think that it will be too time consuming. It is true; it takes time but oh, how you will reap the benefits. Let *Me* teach you how to enjoy the presence of your *Savior* and *Redeemer*. Just find a quiet place with no distractions, no noise, and possibly no interruptions. Then come and reside in this place and offer up worship, praise, and prayer. *I* will come to you in spirit because *I* am *Spirit*. Sit with *Me* for a while and enjoy *My Holy Presence*. Take a moment and be still and listen for that small voice declaring *the Word of the Lord*. *I* will speak to all *My* children if only they take the time to listen. In this hurried world, time is very precious to them. When they learn to share their time with *Me*, they will see wondrous things take place. So come and find that secret place for you to meet and converse.

My children, if you could only imagine the things *I* have in store for those who love the *Lord* with all their heart, mind, and spirit. You, *My* children, can only fantasize what *I* have in store for all *My* believers. If and when *My* children choose to spend time with *Me* and in *My Presence*, they will begin to see marvelous wonders. It's a choice everyone must make on their won. You choose and set up a routine to spend some time with *Me* and build a relationship. You see, *My* children, you can only imagine the benefits of sitting in the presence of your *Heavenly Father* and all the blessings *I* have in store for those who choose to come into *My Presence*. What you will behold in *My Presence* is peace, understanding, and joy unspeakable. In the presence of the *Lord*, you will find a friend and comforter. *I* am *Jehovah-Rapha*—the *Lord* that heals thee. *I* am *Jehovah-Jireh*—your provider. *I Jehovah-El Shaddai* who is able to handle all situations. Most of all, *I* am *Jehovah-Shalom*—your peace. Above all else, you will see the love *I* have for all *My* people. They can't truly experience it until they sit in *My Presence* and enjoy a complete relationship with the *God* of the universe. *I* am here, and to all of *Mine*, *I* say come!

To all who are lost, come into *My* outstretched arms; receive *Me* and *My* plan of salvation. Come and let *Me* wrap *My* arms around you and surround you with love, peace, and joy which the world cannot offer nor understand. *I* see your heartaches, and *I* long to comfort you, but first, you must make a choice of acceptance. Let *Me* be your constant companion, closest friend, confiding confidant, healer of your soul, and altogether loving *Father*. You that are lost must make the choice. When you partake of what the world offers and are not satisfied, then come to *Me*. *I* will satisfy all your needs and desires, but first, you must choose. I'm here waiting patiently to embrace you and cover you with love and grace. *My* yoke is easy, and *My* burdens are light, so all who are lost, *I* say *come*. Don't put it off until tomorrow because you have no guarantee of another day. Now is the time for all who are lost to come and accept *My* salvation!

ollowers of the *Lord Jesus Christ*, do you follow after *Me* and *My Word*, or do you follow after the things the world has to offer? There's no satisfaction found in the material things of the world. They will only bring you pain, suffering, depression, hate, misery, violence, and finally destruction of your soul, mind, and body. Now when you follow after *Me* and *My Holy Word*, you will reap the blessings of joy, peace, and everlasting love and hope; also including the benefit of eternity with your *Lord* in *Heaven*. So you see, it is more profitable in *My* kingdom than the earthly realm. The things of *Heaven* are forever and ever until the end of time. The material things of the earth are for only a season, temporary; seeking after the worldly attractions can only bring heartaches. Seeking the things of *God* will bring you joy unexplainable. You will find peace that the world does not know. You will experience agape love and will be called a child of *Mine*.

MAY 30, 2016

People of faith, when you choose to follow after *Me*, do not look back at the things behind you. Looking back means you have regrets. Instead, look forward to your life with *Christ* in the center. Life is like a half circle without *Jesus*. The circle is completed when the *Lord and Savior* is in the midst of it. Live your life with *Me* first, and all else in your life will fall into the path *I* have set before you. You can do nothing on your own; only with *My* strength can *My* people accomplish the things before them. Call upon *My* name, and *I* will be there in spirit. *I* am your righteousness of *God*. *I* am your burnt offering, and by *My* stripes, you are healed. Realize, *My* people, through your salvation, you become a child of the living *God*. *My Spirit* indwells in you. You are more than a conqueror because the enemy has been defeated by the blood of the *Lamb* and *the Word* of your testimony. So go forth and proclaim the precious *Holy Word of God* and watch the blessings come forth.

MAY 31, 2016

People, people, people, what don't you understand about the plan of salvation of your *Lord*? Is it taking up your cross daily and following after *Me*? This means that following after *Me* would involve suffering and hardships. Be blessed and comforted for doing that which is right, for yours is then the kingdom of *Heaven*. People, only those who endure until the end will inherit the kingdom of *God*. *My Word* is going forth continually by ministers' say of the gospel and by *My* chosen ones. Yet many say, "*I* don't have time for this now." Listen, *My* people, time is extremely short before *My* coming back for *My* bride. People, stop and think while running to and fro; the things you are following after now are only temporary. The things I'm offering are eternal. Look at your world now as evil is showing itself more and more. Beware that you don't get entrapped by false teachers. There is only one true *God*. Take up your cross daily and follow after *Me*. You will have suffering and hardships, but you will be blessed and comforted for doing that which is right. For yours is then the kingdom of *Heaven*. You will give up some things, and then you will reap joy, peace, and love. Those are *My* gifts for you. Come and seek what *I* have in store for those who come into *My* kingdom and accept *My* salvation. Why, oh why, aren't more people accepting *My* salvation?

Life with *Jesus* in the center makes life complete.

Life without *Jesus*.

The chosen generation! I'm asking of *My* people, "Do you know *Me*?" You know about *Me* and have knowledge of *Me*, but do you know *Me* personally? Take in account the word *know* and its definition. To know someone is spending quality time with an individual, asking questions about them, also sharing your own desires and beliefs. You can share knowledge of family and friends, your cares, likes, and dislikes. This is how you get to know someone. Same is said about getting to know your *Heavenly Father*. Come into *My Presence* and converse with *Me*. *I* enjoy *My* chosen ones coming to *Me* with their daily prayer requests. *I* love it when *My* children choose to spend time with *Me* above all else. Talk with *Me*, sharing your heartfelt desires, your needs, and your pain. *I* am your loving *Father* and will give unto you forgiveness, comfort, peace, and abiding love. Come, and tell *Me* what's in your heart. Share with *Me* at the end of the day. Tell *Me* how your day unfolded. Tell *Me* how you helped spread *My Word* and how you helped someone in need. At bedtime, don't forget to spend time with *Me* in prayer, asking for a peaceful sleep and heavenly dreams. Thankfulness and praise for each day is greatly accepted. Be blessed, *My* children.

JUNE 2, 2016

For *My* people, the words in a song say, "Let your little light shine." *I* say, "Let your beacon shine for all the lost to see and be drawn into its marvelous light." Let the joy and the presence of the *Lord* in you shine for all to see. Let them see the glory of the newborn *King*. Let *My Holy Presence* go forth from you, *My* people, into this darkened world. Let your beacon light be a witness to the oppressed and all who are in need of your guiding light. *My* people, be equipped by *My Spirit* to answer questions from those who seek answers and for those in need of prayer. Stay focused, *My* chosen ones, on the mission *I* have called you to do. You are the light for this lost generation. You are their hope by showing the love, compassion, and goodness of your *Heavenly Father*. You have been prepared for a mission as this. Take heed and don't be overcome by the enemy. Put him in his place under your feet. Go forth and let your beacon light shine for all the world to see. Remember, you, *My* people, are the light of the world!

My children, *I* hear your prayers and your cries of pain and suffering. *I* will answer your prayers when you call upon *My* name. Your answers may not be in your time because *My* timing may not be as yours. *My* ways may not be your ways. Be careful as to what you pray and ask. Ask something in *My* name, and *I* will grant it. Some prayers are answered immediately while others are gradual and take time. Some healings are immediate while others are slowly evolving. Yet some may take a long time to manifest. Circumstances can sometimes interfere with healings. If you don't seem to get an answer to your prayer, keep asking. Be thankful and grateful in all your requests of prayer. Your gratitude is a blessing to *Me*. *I* adore it when *My* children show thanksgiving to *Me* even in pain and sorrow. Thank *Me* in all your situations for *I* am merciful.

JUNE 6, 2016

*M*y children, whenever strife and complications in life arise, seek *Me* above all else. Pray about everything, and in everything, give thanks. Prayer is the great problem solver and the greatest comfort. Because when in prayer, you are giving *Me* all your anxieties, cares, and woes. In prayer, that means you trust everything to *Me*. When asking in prayer for something or for someone and an answer does not come immediately, don't be disheartened. Prayers are answered not according to what you desire but what *I* foresee and what *I* deem necessary. All prayers are heard and answered accordingly. *I* see what's best for *My* children. If your prayer is not answered right away, keep praying and seeking for *My* will to be done in your life. Above all else, always pray about everything. Be persistent and faithful in your prayer time, repeating unanswered prayers and seeking *My* will.

JUNE 7, 2016

To all *My* people, are you good servants? Do you wisely distribute the gifts and blessings that have been given to you? The gifts which have been given to you are to be used wisely for the kingdom of *God*. Whether it be finances or blessings of earthly things, use them to glorify your *Lord*. Do not hoard or covet any earthly thing this world has to offer. Covet only the things in the kingdom of *God*. *I* bless all *My* people with many blessings. It's up to them on how to use them. Take great care and consideration, also a lot of prayer in guiding you in regard to your blessings. Give to those in need, whether it be food, finances, clothing, or a word from the *Lord*. Share all *I* have given to you, and you will be blessed a hundredfold. Give and it shall be given unto you—good measure, pressed down and shaken together, and running over. Also remember to tithe on all your earning. It helps the kingdom of *God*. Be faithful, *My* people, and manage your blessings well!

JUNE 8, 2016

To all *My* people, hear what *the Word of God* is saying! Be diligent in your worship, prayer, and thanksgiving. Be mindful of others. Upon seeing someone in need, take the time to pray with them. Show them mercy and grace that your *Father* has shown you. Then listen to their problems and share the plan of salvation. Explain the love and forgiveness that *I* made available through the sacrifice of *My Son* on the cross. This plan of salvation is for all who will accept it. It's freely given for all. The choice is up to each individual. Tell the people when they accept *My* salvation, they will be endowed with *My Holy Spirit. He* will reside in them and will lead and guide them through their pathway of life. Listen to the inner voice of *My Holy Spirit* when *He* speaks. Sometimes the *Holy Spirit* will nudge you. Sometimes *He* will correct you. *He* is very persistent and won't let go. Whatever *My* people do, don't give up listening to *My Spirit.*

JUNE 9, 2016

To *My* precious, loving children, come and sit in the *Presence* of your *Heavenly Father*. Let the eyes of your heart be open to *My Words*. Let your ears hear what *the Word of God* is speaking. Come expecting, and you will receive. Come with a grateful and thankful heart and receive blessings. Come and just be still and know that *I* am *God*. *I* am here waiting for all that love *Me* to come and sit with *Me*. *My* precious, loving ones, when you choose to sit in *My Presence* and enjoy *My* fellowship, it does your *Father's* heart good. *I* do love *My* children, and yet they don't have time for *Me*. It seems other things are more important. Why can't you, *My* children, know what it means for you to come to *Me*? Don't just wait until a problem arises and then come seeking *Me*—to which *I* am always there waiting even if it's just to solve a problem. *I* so want *My* children to come, and let us enjoy each other's presence. Come, *My* precious ones, your *Heavenly Father* is waiting with outstretched arms longing for *His* children.

JUNE 10, 2016

To all believers, the time is coming in which you must state what you believe. As your world is changing its views, some of *My* people are also changing to go with the crowd. Real followers of *Christ* will stand firm and will not be moved. People, your faith and beliefs are going to be tempted and tested. You must remain faithful to *the Word of God* and all its teachings. *The Word* is true and does not change to suit an individual's interpretation. Believe only what's in the Holy Scriptures and no other. When speaking to nonbelievers, be able to support what you say with the Bible. This way, the nonbelievers will understand what *the Word of God* is saying as it is backed up by the Bible. Let *My* indwelling *Spirit* help you and guide you in reaching the lost. Sometimes nonbelievers know sayings from the Bible, and they change the true meanings for their own benefit. *My Word* is true and will never change for anyone. *My Word* is forever and ever.

JUNE 11, 2016

Children of the *Most High*, consider how blessed you are and be willing to share your blessings with others that are lost. Help those in dire need! Always be willing to help anyone, anytime or anywhere. The needs people have can be overwhelming. Always try to understand what they require most from you. *I* want that *My* people be givers. Not only of time, money, and material things, but also be willing to tell of your blessings and henceforth where they came. Share the love of your *Father*. Explain by the many blessings from *God* that you are able to help others. Speak to them of the marvelous compassion and love that your *Father* has for all mankind. The lost are believing in the god of the world, and it will lead them to destruction. They will always have a lack and void in their heart that only *I*, their *Creator*, can fill *My* children. Keep praying and lend a helping hand to those in need. Keep reaching out to the lost, and gently guide them toward the direction of *Heaven* and into the kingdom of the living *God*.

Ministers of the gospel, by looking around in your world, you see all the lost running about not knowing where they are going. You see, the lost don't realize their need of salvation or their need for a *Savior*. The unbelievers are so deep in sin; they don't fathom that there is someone who can save them and pull them out of the miry pit into *My* marvelous light. *My* heart breaks when *I* see all the lost people worshipping idols of the enemy, being misled by false teachings and false witnesses. Some of the unbelievers have went even so far as to have their own bible published. The teachings of the prophets were changed for their own misguided values. Woe to all who change *the Word of God* for their own lifestyle or misuse. *My Word* is true and will stand through the end of time. Before ministering to the lost souls, pray their ears, and the eyes of their heart will be opened for your words. Then speak to them of life after death. Ask them where they think they will spend eternity. Some don't even believe in life after the grave. Use *My Holy Word*, and show them there is life after the grave. It's just a matter of choice as to where they will spend eternity.

My Child,

As you are enjoying family and friends, remember to whom you belong. You belong to the family of *God*. You are a daughter of the *Most High*. Don't forget to shine for your *Father in Heaven*. You are a representation of your *Lord* on earth. Think what *Jesus* would do in this situation. Before speaking about anyone, think: Will what *I* say edify this person or be harmful to them? Don't speak harm to or about anyone. Your tongue is a powerful weapon. It speaks life or death. *I* can help you tame your tongue. *My* child, honor your *Heavenly Father* with praise, honor, and glory. Listen and don't prejudge anyone or any circumstances. I'm in control of all situations and of your life. Behold, *My* daughter, and be aware of the great gift *I* have given to you to use for *My* glory. Enjoy this time and speak of *Me* often. Others are watching, so be an example for all the world to see.

Love,
Your *Heavenly Father*

JUNE 15, 2016

People of the world, whether you are people of faith or the lost of the world, because you don't see things happening in the real world, is that cause for your nonbelief? You don't see the wind, and yet it blows; you can feel its force. Not everything is tangible and still it can be effective. People of faith, you don't see *My* hand working in the lives of your loved ones. So you doubt! *I'm* working, and yet it may take time for *My* plans to manifest. Lost people don't believe unless they see miracles, signs, and wonders they witness themselves. Seeing is not believing. Oh, you of little faith. Some see and still don't believe. *My* handiwork is in every living thing. *I* created all breathing life forms in the universe. So the lost ask for signs, and the signs of *My* creation are all around them, and still, they won't believe. The lost people have been so indoctrinated with the enemy's ideas and can't see the goodness of *God* all around them. Open the eyes of your hearts, people of the world.

JUNE 16, 2016

To all the inhabitants of the world, people with different beliefs choose to harm and seek to destroy others that don't have their same ideas and beliefs. They choose weapons of war as in a battleground. They believe by the taking of lives, they can change the opinions of others. Nothing gets solved by the taking of human lives, whether it be children or adults. One act of violence brings on another and so on. The root of the acts of violence is Satan. He has misled humankind for centuries. This lost generation who have chosen violence to settle their views don't understand about humanity. All *My* creations have been given a will. They choose whom they serve. Some choose to follow the ways of the world. It results in conflict because not all views agree. Then you have someone who doesn't see eye to eye and sets out to change others by violence. Nothing is accomplished by violence. *My* people have been equipped with weapons of warfare to use in the battle against Satan. It's the armor of *God*. *My* heart breaks for all the ones hurt by acts of violence. Bring *Me* your hurts and sorrows!

JUNE 17, 2016

*M*y people, do you have a thorn in the flesh? Something that hinders you or keeps you from your daily routines. Sometimes afflictions and thorns of the flesh are allowed, not to hinder or stop you but to humble you and bring you closer to your *Lord* in prayer. As with the Apostle Paul, he prayed three times for the removal of the thorn in his flesh. *My* answer to him was: "*My* grace is sufficient for you." *My* people, do not use your disability or affliction for pity or sympathy. Use it as a badge of honor, showing that the *Lord* can use everyone to further the kingdom. No matter the affliction of a person, they can still be of important use for the *Lord's* purpose. Even being in confinement, you can serve and work for the glory of your *Savior*. The Apostle Paul's thorn in the flesh never stopped his work for the kingdom. Sometimes *My* people will use an affliction as an excuse to avoid studying *My Word* or praying for people. Rejoice, *My* people, in all things and give thanksgiving to your *Creator*. Worship and praise to the *Lord* all you Christian people of the world. Don't let anything hinder or stop you from serving your *Lord Jesus*. Your rewards will be bountiful.

My brethren, *I* am the *Good Shepherd*! All those who accept *My* plan of salvation become *My* sheep. Being a *Good Shepherd*, *I* am always watching, listening, and protecting *My* flock. *I* will lead and guide them with *the Word of God*. They will feed on *My Holy Word*; it is food for their soul. *My* sheep will know *My* voice and will follow after *Me*. The pathway sometimes may seem treacherous, and they may feel like they can't go on; it's then *I* will pick them up and carry them. They will feel safe in *My* loving arms. *My* sheep can depend on *Me* for comfort, protection, guidance, and a heart full of love, grace, and compassion. *I* love all the sheep in *My* flock, and *I* know when one is in trouble and needs *My* attention. All they have to do is call upon *My* name, and *I* will be in their midst. In *My* flock, there are sheep of many colors. Also, they are of different sizes, shapes, and sizes. You see, none of *My* sheep are the same, and no two are alike. Each one has different qualities and needs. These are *My* sheep now but once were lost and in need of a *Savior* and a *Good Shepherd* to point the way to *Heaven*. *I* say to all the lost sheep of the world, come and let *Me* be your *Good Shepherd*. *I* say come!

JUNE 20, 2016

*M*y people, why are you continually complaining about one thing or another? Do you not know you are a blessed generation? Count your blessings one by one. If you woke up this morning and got out of bed, that's a blessing. How many people that are bedridden would love to be able to get out of bed? How many are grateful just to wake up? Some pass from the life without waking up and into their death. If you have two feet and legs to stand on, be blessed. How many people have lost their limbs one way or another? If you have two arms to hold someone, you are blessed. Because of sickness or injuries, people lose their arms and hands. You that have eyes to see the world around, you are blessed. There are those that are blind, and yet they see more clearly than ones with eyesight. There are those who can speak and yet remain silent. *My* people, don't complain or groan! You have a lesser reason to complain than the lost. You possess blessings immeasurable. You are a chosen generation. Count your blessings and thank your *Heavenly Father* for the blessings you do have.

JUNE 21, 2016

Dear friends, are you true friends of the living *God*? Do you have an intimate relationship with your *Creator*? *I* call you *My* friends when you come to *Me* for salvation. Then it's up to you to build a relationship with *Me*. It requires spending time with *Me* in prayer and just sitting quietly in *My Presence*. Friendship is a precious commodity rarely used in your world. It is love and trust for individuals. Spending time together is a requirement. Sharing problems and solutions, discussing daily activities is a must. It's an all-around getting to know you and how you perceive issues in your life. If you have one close friend, you are blessed more than silver and gold. A true friend is more valuable than diamonds. Friends may come in different sizes, shapes, ages, and colors. The most precious of all is that they are always available when you are in need, no matter the time day or night. Knowing you can count on them is a comfort. Now *I* say again, are you friends with the living *God*? If not, come and share with *Me*. *I* am always waiting for you!

JUNE 24, 2016

*M*y children, look toward the sky, for your *Redeemer* draws nigh. The rewarder of those who diligently seek *Him* is coming soon very soon. Are you, *My* beloved, ready to meet your *Lord and Savior*? Are you resting in the knowledge of *His Holy Word*? Are you seeking forgiveness for known and unknown sin in your life? Are you constantly praying for your enemies and all the lost of the world? *My* children, be on the alert and watchful for the coming of your *Lord*! *I* am coming for a people that are praying and interceding for all those that are lost in sin. In your world today, there are a lot of unbelievers. They are following the god of their world, not knowing that it will lead to eternal damnation. Some lost of your world may not know that there is an alternative. It's up to *My* children to go forth and teach and speak of *the Word of God* and the salvation that is available upon request. There are so many whom even in this electronic era have not heard of *the Word of God*. Some may have heard of the distorted versions which are used for their own lifestyle. Speak of *My Holy Word* which is true and cannot be changed for man's way of living. It remains the same through centuries and will be so until the end of time. So, *My* people, are you patiently waiting for the return of your *Lord and Savior*?

JUNE 25, 2016

*M*y children, are you a new creation? Are you truly born again? Do you have the life and nature of *God* in your spirit? Do you purposely walk in the light and not darkness in your life? Do you acknowledge that *God* lives in you? Does *He* instruct, lead, and guide you? Are you truly a child of the *Most High God* with *His* wisdom and *Holy Spirit* guiding you in your pathway of life? Do you give daily unto *Him* the praise and worship worthy of a *King*? *My* children should daily declare that your *Heavenly Father* lives in you. *My* children can call out for *Me*, and *I* in no way will cast them away. They can call upon *My* name at anytime, day or night in any circumstances or situation, and *I* will hear. They can walk with the knowledge that *God* is on their side. If *God* is for you, who can be against you? Child of *Mine*, *I* have written your name in the palm of *My* hand. Do you have *My* name written upon your heart?

JUNE 27, 2016

*M*y brethren, do you love *Me*? Do you seek *Me* and *My Presence* daily? Do you read and study *My Holy Word* daily? If this is so, then *I* can call you *My* faithful and *My* chosen ones. Stay in communion with *Me* daily and in *My* will for your life. You didn't choose *Me*. *I* have chosen you. *I* have great plans for your life. *I* need you to be prayed up and prepared for what is lying ahead. Come, *My* brethren, and let *Me* show you what *I* have in store for those whom are faithful to *the Word of God*. The blessings of *Heaven* are waiting for those who hold on until the end. *My* brethren, you must choose this day whom you will serve and remain true to. Don't slip back into lukewarmness, or *I* will spew you out of *My* mouth. *I* desire you to be on fire for your *Lord* and *His* plan of salvation for mankind. Be faithful in prayer and *My Word*, and the enemy can't get a foothold! Don't stray; keep your mind set on *Me*.

JUNE 28, 2016

To all *My* followers, in your daily Christian walk, you will be tried, tested, and tempted. Stay true to your belief and faith. Remain loyal, faithful, and totally committed to your *Lord Jesus Christ*. In your world, even daily routines can become trying. Depend on *My* indwelling *Holy Spirit* for guidance and comfort. Call upon *Him* in any situation, and *He* is as close as your next breath. *My* followers need to depend more on *My Holy Spirit* and less on the knowledge and beliefs of others. Someone will always have an opinion when a problem arises. Be gracious and politely inform them that you only listen to the inner voices of *God's Holy Spirit*. Some then will think you different. So be it! Stay forever loyal to your inner voices of *My Holy Spirit*. *He* will never leave nor forsake you even when the going gets rough. That's when *He* is more effective. Listen *My* followers to the prompting of the *Holy Spirit*. *He* will lead you to a closer walk with *Heavenly Father*.

JUNE 29, 2016

People of faith, *I* am the vinedresser and the one true vine. You, *My* people, are the branches. Are your branches bringing forth fruit, or are you barren? *I* will continually prune you daily, checking for much fruit. Upon not finding fruit, you will be cut off. People of faith, start declaring *the Word of the Lord*. In your daily living, speak often of your *Heavenly Father* to all you encounter. That's helping to spread *My* gospel and being a true messenger of your faith. True believers who love *the Word of God* are eager to share it with others. The more you share, the more fruit you produce. The more fruit, the more branches. *My* people, the time is now for all *My* chosen ones to step up and step out against all the wrongs of the world. Don't be afraid to address issues that are against your beliefs and faith. It's easy to sit back and say what you believe, and it's entirely different to go out into your world and declare, "Thus saith the *Lord*, 'People of faith in your own families and amongst friends, declare that one day every knee will bow and every tongue will confess that *Jesus Christ* is *Lord* over the whole universe!'"

JUNE 30, 2016

To all people of the world, *I* love all *My* people (my creations) but have a special love for the ones that belong to the family of *God*. *I* have a special fatherly love for those that follow after *Me* and the things of *My* kingdom. *My* chosen ones upon their salvation were endowed with the *Holy Spirit*. That's *My* gift to those who have accepted *My* plan of salvation. Virtues of the *Holy Spirit* are love, joy, peace, patience, kindness, goodness, faithfulness, gentleness, and self-control. *My* people, do not suppress the *Spirit* within you. *He* is an all-around comforter. *He* is *My Spirit* residing inside each believer. Be open to *His* guidance, and *He* will lead you to a closer relationship with your *Heavenly Father* by instilling a stronger desire to know *Me* and *My Word* more and more. *He* guides believers in prayer and intercession. Come and talk with *Me* and enjoy the family of *God*.

JULY 2, 2016

To all the lost, you are following after all the wrong things of the world. You idolize material things, electronic devices, man-made items, and wearable. You desire to be something you are not. You seek after worldly desires and worldly pleasures. They are only temporary satisfactions for your real wants. Then the lost go from one extreme to another seeking after men of *God* and their preaching and teachings. When the only thing to seek after is him, *the Word of God*, and *His* plan of salvation. By doing so, people will learn the real truth and all the hypocrisy and lies coming forth. You must seek after the good in everyone. Don't let yourself get so wrapped up in worldly matters that you forget to seek after heavenly matters. The kingdom of *God* is what matters. So to the lost, *I* say follow after the things of the world, and they will lead you to eternal hellfire and separation from *God* forever. Seek *Me* and *My* kingdom for your eternal home.

My children, today, your country honors freedom from bondage of an oppressing nation! *I* have offered you freedom, freedom from the bondage of sin. Yet the lost would rather live in the bondage of sin and be miserable than to accept *My* plan of salvation. People, what will it take to turn away from your wicked ways? Will it take an earth-shattering experience or life-threatening situation? In most of your lives, you have already had this happen, and you have lived through it. What then will it take for you to turn your life over to *Me*? *I* am waiting patiently with outstretched arms for all who will respond. One day, *My* patience will end and so will your life. Death can come in a moment's time; it may be an accident or of natural causes. You may not have time to repent. So the time is now for all to come and know their *Creator* and all *I* have for those who accept *My* salvation. The sins and violence in your world should cause everyone to take a look at what's in store for a nation without *God*. You cannot change these things in your world. They will change only with the prayers offered up to *God* and the repentance of sinners. Heed *My* warnings!

Friends of *God*, come into *My Presence*, friends of *Mine*, and share with *Me* all your problems. *I* long to listen to *My* children and friends sharing with *Me* all that pertains to them whether it be a problem, a concern, or something that they need help with. *I* am a friend that sticks closer than a brother, willing always to listen, encourage, and give helpful advice. Also *I* can help in many other ways. *I* need all *My* followers to bring their likes and dislikes, problems, and concerns before *Me* asking for *My* help. It's these times that develop into a trusted relationship. But you see, *I* need for *My* friends to ask for help from the one true friend in solving their problems. Only with *My* help can it be overcome. On your own, you just struggle, but with *My* help and encouragement, everything is possible. Be a good cheer, *My* family of friends and followers. *I* have overcome the world. You see, you are in good hands!

Child of *Mine*, I've heard your prayers and requests! You've asked, "Why are some people healed while others come home to be with you in paradise?" These questions, *My* children, were asked frequently. What *I* can say is before a person is born, their days on earth are numbered. When their time is up, there's nothing doctors can do. The person's fate rests in the hands of the *Creator*. Sometimes the reason for not receiving a miracle of healing may be due to the person's condition of their heart and the relationship with their *Savior*. Child of *Mine*, you do what *I've* called you to do. Keep praying and believing for those in need of healing. That's what you are endowed to do. Leave the divine decisions about miracles and whom gets healed to your *Heavenly Father*. You, *My* child, are to be faithful in honoring *Me* and *My Holy Word*. Keep reading and studying, also interceding on behalf of those in need. The greatest healing of all time is for a person to be welcomed into *Heaven*!

JULY 7, 2016

Christians around the world, do you love *Me*? If your answer is yes, then go forth and help the lost sheep find their way to the kingdom of *God*. The fields are ripe awaiting for the harvest to come. *My* people, what are you waiting for? In your reluctance, you are letting the lost sheep fall into the hands of the enemy. Go forth about *the Word of God*. *My* people think because of this electronic age of gadgets that everyone has heard of *the Word of God*. Don't make any misguided assumptions in regard to others' knowledge of *the Word*. Tell the people of *God* and *His* many blessings and promises. Tell of all the miracles in the Bible. Some of the lost believe they are being punished for past sins, yet others believe that the name *God* to be called on only in time of need. Tell them upon salvation, they are forgiven of all sins, past and present. That *My Holy Spirit* comes and resides in them, leading and guiding their lives if they will only listen to *Him*. Go *My* people and preach to all the lost of the nations. Tell them of the love awaiting them with the one and only true *God*!

JULY 8, 2016

Part 1

Chosen ones, *I* am patiently waiting for *My* chosen ones to reach out more to the unsaved ones. The harvest is ripe, and yet there's only a few who are bold enough to go forth and declare, "The time is now for those who will harken unto *the Word of the Lord*." Speak in the streets of your cities in meetings, in gatherings, conferences, anywhere there are people. Speak of the love of *God*. Your world is in turmoil. It's in need of a *God* of love and mercy. If the people of the world would turn from their wicked ways and seek forgiveness, then *I* would heal their land. The people of the world think they can solve all the problems on their own. What the countries of the world need now is to hear from *God Almighty* in a thunderous way so that they will turn from their wicked ways. Seems people would understand that all the violence erupting means the enemy is using everything to promote his agenda. What Christians need to declare that *God* is still on the throne and still in control. What the world needs is more people seeking the face of *God* and praying and interceding on behalf of all the lost.

Part 2

Nations of the world, the Israelite people were in bondage to the Egyptians for 400 years. *I* sent *My* Prophet Moses to lead *My* people out of bondage and into the promised land. Long ago in your land, people of different color were brought to your land as slaves. Many years later, they regained their freedom from slavery, and yet still today, they are persecuted because of the color of their skin, nationality, and religious beliefs. In the creation, all mankind was created in the image of *God*. Persecution and racism are horrific in themselves, but to kill or injure someone because of their color is wrong. It's the attack of the enemy, bringing dissension amongst *My* people. *My* people, do not sit back and allow this. All *My* people are equal in the eyes of *God*. *I* do not look outwardly at people but at their hearts. *My* people, wake up and see what's happening in the world and help to stop it. Stop judging or criticizing because of someone's skin color or nationality. Help stop the hatred of your fellow men by showing love and respect to all *God's* creations.

JULY 10, 2016

Christian of the world, if you really are followers of the *Lord Jesus Christ* and *My* teachings, then it's time for all Christians to stand up for their faith. Take a bold stand against all the violence and hatred of mankind. *I* see all the rebellion, hatred, and all the violence against each other. This does not accomplish anything except more hatred and more violence. It's a vicious circle fed by those that don't know love. People with authority use hatred for their own plight not realizing the pain and suffering it causes to those left behind.

My Holy Word declares to love your neighbor as yourself. It does not declare to love only those that you choose are worthy of your love or if that person is a different race, creed, or religion. Neighbor implies everyone whether it be people living beside you or when in pursuit of your daily living, any person you come in contact with. You are, as Christians, to show love and respect to all mankind.

The Word of God declares for all of Christ followers to love mankind in such a way that they will know the love of the *Father*. Rebellious people need to realize who is at the root of all the hatred and racism! It has all started from the enemy of all Christians—Satan! *My* followers can overcome with love for their fellowman.

JULY 11, 2016

C hildren of *God*, you live in a society that worships all kinds of idols. Some are living while others are deceased. You may say you don't worship any idols! And *I* say anything that takes you away from spending time with *Me* is an idol, anything that comes first in your life is an idol. *I* am a jealous *God* and perceive all things. *My* desire is for *My* children to be needful of the heavenly things and not depend on earthly things. *Heavenly* things are eternal while earthly or material things are temporary. Keep your mind set on your *Heavenly Father* and the things of the kingdom. Make *Me* first in everything in your life. Upon rising from sleep, your first thought should be of your *Heavenly Father*. Do not let the things of the world concern you, *My* children. When all looks hopeless, that's when I'm working effortlessly. Keep believing *My* chosen ones and keep praying in faith for all nations and nationalities. One day, there will be peace for all mankind, but until that time, there will be trials and tribulations. Just remember to keep your mind and thoughts on the spiritual ways and not on the ways of the world. Stay true to *Me*, *My* people!

JULY 12, 2016

My children, when will you understand what *I* am saying when *I* say, "Come into *My Presence*?" *I* don't desire for *My* children to only speak of *Me* or to *Me* occasionally. *I* desire and want *My* precious children to come before *Me* daily, disregarding everything else and sit in *My Presence*. Find a quiet place and come with praise and thanksgiving. Come to honor you *Heavenly Father*. Welcome *Me*, and *I* will come and sit with you. When will you, *My* children, realize that all your *Heavenly Father* requires is to love you and wants you to spend time with *Him*. *My* children find more important things to occupy their time. *I* am pushed aside to be called upon in time of need. *I* want to be involved in all aspects of *My* people's lives, especially when things are going wrong. Come into *My Presence* and tell *Me* all that's hurting you. *I* will give you comfort. Come to *Me* when in distress, and *I* will give you peace. Come unto *Me* when others betray you, and *I* will give you love and forgiveness. *I* understand betrayal because *I* was betrayed and died on the cross and rose on the third day. When on the cross, *I* said, "*Father*, forgive them they know not what they do." Come to *Me* with your tears and let *Me* wipe them away. *My* children, come into *My Presence* and experience all that *I* have for you. When *God* is for you, who can be against you? If you abide in *Me* and *My Word* abides in you, you can ask anything in *My* name, and it shall be given!

To Whom It May Concern,

Do not be saddened or bitter about the passing of your daughter! Remember, *I* also know the heartache because I, too, lost someone *I* loved deeply. *My Son*, take heart and rejoice, *My* child, that when your daughter became ill, she rededicated her life to *Me*. So now, she is in her eternal home. No more sickness and no more pains. Rejoice that one day you will be reunited with her in glory. Be comforted with the memories and her children she left behind. Encompass her family and comfort them in their time of mourning. *I* send this message to you for your peace of mind and endurance. Be blessed, *My* child, and fill yourself with the love of all your Christian brothers and sisters. Keep praying for all those that are lost.

Your *Heavenly Father*

To all *My* followers, the day has come for all the believers of the world to stand up and declare *the Word of the Lord*! Don't concern yourselves with whom will be offended when you speak of *Jesus Christ*. It's up to *My* people to get you to belong in whom you serve. Witness to all those you encounter. Stay faithful, *My* people, because it is very easy to get entrapped by all the things of the world. Don't let them draw you away and into worldly opinions. Stay true to your beliefs and don't waver. You will be blessed and greatly rewarded for your faithfulness. *My* followers, the time is now for all Christians to come into one accord and declare your beliefs and rights. You as *My* children have privileges, equal rights to the throne of *God*. Use this gift and seek *Me* above all else!

JULY 16, 2016

*M*y daughter, you are one of *My* many daughters. You are special to *Me* as all *My* children are special when doing their *Father's* will. You, *My* child, remain faithful in your reading *My Word* and spending time with *Me. I* know, *My* daughter, that you are weak when it comes to praying for others. Stay in *My Word*, and *I* will make you a prayer warrior. The more you pray, the more the words will flow. Do not hinder *My Holy Spirit*! *He* is *My* gift to you. Remember, *My* daughter, you have the mind of *Christ*. You, like *My* other children, don't realize or understand that they have the same power in them that was in *My Son Jesus*. When *My* children upon realizing this and start to see miracles, use the power to stop the enemy. This power was given to each and every believer upon their salvation. Do not abuse or misuse this power. It's best used in glorifying your *Heavenly Father*. It's *My* desire, *My* child, for you and all *My* children to be bold and forthright in regard to witnessing to the lost. Go into the world, *My* sons and daughters, and bring in the lost sheep into the heavenly kingdom. *My* daughter, watch what you say as your words go forth. Let them be blessings, not cursing. Let them bring healing, comfort, and love from your *Heavenly Father*! Don't speak harshly of anyone or about any of *My* creations. *My Holy Presence* abides in you. Guard it carefully with honor and respect.

S aints of *God*, do you acknowledge *Me* before family and friends? Do you declare that you love *Me* with all your spirit, soul, and body? Do you tell all those you come in contact with that you are a child of the *Most High God*? These are the questions you as saints should be asking yourself daily. Ask yourself this daily: "Have *I* done all *I* could do to further *God's* kingdom?" If any one answer is no, then, *My* child, you need to make some changes in your lifestyle. *My* saints, *I* can't impress on you enough how important it is for all *My* people to declare *the Word of the Lord*, giving testimonies of what *God* has done for you. Give thanks in everything. Count your blessings before all to see. Let them see the love you possess for your *Heavenly Father*. There are people of your world starving for peace of mind, a joyful heart, and love unspeakable—love of a *Father* they may not have ever known. Tell them, saints, about the *God* of the universe who came and died for their salvation and an eternal home in Heaven!

JULY 19, 2016

*M*y brethren, in your pathway of life, you will come across sin and sinners. You on your own cannot change the individuals! Just be silently praying for them that they would turn from their wicked ways and turn to *Me*. Remember, *I* love the sinner, not the sin, so should you! Do not cease; just keep continuing to pray for them. Sin is more rampant now and will get even worse until *I* come again. Some you can convince to change from their wicked ways, and yet others will continue in their sins. Without knowing *My Word*, most don't realize what sin is. Those participating in sin believe that there are no repercussions or punishment. Most believe this: Live while you can live to the fullest with no consequences for the things you do. There will be a time when all will answer for their lifestyles and the things they speak. One day, every knee will bow, and every tongue will confess *Jesus* is *Lord* of all creations. *He* is a rewarder of those who diligently seek him.

JULY 20, 2016

My people, there are so many teachings in the world. It's hard to know what to believe. *My* born-again believers possess the indwelling *Holy Spirit*. *My Spirit*! Listen to him, people, and *He* will lead and guide you in all truths. If something doesn't sound right or feel right, then it's the spirit of the living *God* showing you that this teaching is wrong. Be very observant when someone is sharing a word of knowledge. Make sure it lines up with *the Word of God*. Everything including words of knowledge, prophetic sayings, prophesies must all be in line with the *Holy Word of God*. If not, delete them *I* thought life. In the world, there are people professing "Thus saith the *Lord*." Carefully examine all sayings and teachings with the *Holy Word*. *My* people, if you stay in *My Word* and *My Word* stays in you, you will be able (with *My Holy Spirit*) to distinguish what is true and what is false. This is why *I* say to all *My* people to stay in *the Word* daily so you won't be fooled or misguided into the wrong beliefs. Be faithful in *My Word* and in prayer.

JULY 21, 2016

Believers, do you sing songs of praise in your hour of need? Do you call out *My* name when in distress? *My* believers, in stressful situations, remember to call upon your *Lord and Savior*. *I* will remove those chains of oppression that bind *My* people and keep them from the plans *I* have for them. *I* came to deliver all people from bondage! Yet some will continue to carry their burdens. Believers, in your hour of sorrows, sing out praises to your *Lord and King*. Even in the midnight hour, *I* will abide with you and will deliver you from all oppressions. Come to *Me* all who are burdened and heavily laden, and *I* will give you rest. Sing a song of worship and praise. *I* love to hear the praises of *My* people. It's music to *My* ears. Sing all you people and make joyful noises unto your *Heavenly Father*. Bring your praises and worship, and praise your *Savior*. For *He* is good, and *His* mercy is forever.

JULY 22, 2016

Christians, abide in *Me*, and *My Word* abides in you. Then ask anything in *My* name, and it will be given to you. This abiding means to come into *My Presence* and spend time with *Me*, not just a passing thought or small prayer. Most come before *Me* asking for answers to their prayers, not realizing *I* desire for *My* people to sit awhile in *My Presence*. *I* enjoy when *My* people choose to stay awhile with *Me*. *I* can communicate with you through *My* indwelling *Holy Spirit*. Christians, it so pleases your *Father* for *His* chosen ones to come and enjoy a time of worship, praise, and thanksgiving in quiet time with the *Creator* of the universe. *I* am always available for *My* people to come and abide with *Me*. Now is the time for all Christians to abide in *My Holy Word* and let it be food for thought and for you spirit, body, and soul. Let *My* words permit everything in your body. Let your thoughts be of *the Word of God*. Let your praises be heard. Come and abide with *Me*. *I* say come.

Believers, you not only need to read and study *My Word* but must act upon it. Put it in use daily. Don't be like the hypocrites, saying one thing and doing another. Say what you mean, and mean what you say. Don't teach things of *My Word* to others unless you are willing to abide by them. *My Word* is true and will never change. All believers should be true to their faith and belief, working earnestly to bring *the Word* to all the world. There are people dying and going to hell that have not been told about the plan of salvation. Believers, don't rely on others to do the work *I* have called you to do. Behold and brazen and forthcoming with all your encounter. Don't back down. Make your declaration of your faith and *the Word of God*. Speak it in love and compassion to all who will listen. Be willing to listen to other viewpoints and be knowledgeable in *My Holy Word* to explain and answer questions. Believers, it's up to you to bring in the harvest.

*M*y children, when everything seems to be going wrong, *I* will make a way! When the enemy causes bad things to happen, *I* will turn them for your good. *I* will always make a way for you when it seems there's no way. Lean on *Me* when everything is going wrong. By leaning on *Me* means that you trust *Me* to take care of your situation, and take care of it, *I* will! When the enemy sends bad things your way, be of good cheer. *I* have defeated the enemy and overcome the world. *I* can turn all the bad situations around for good for all those who love the *Lord*! In all desperate situations, *I* will always make a way out regardless of what befalls you. *I* am the way, truth, and life. No one comes to the *Father* except *My Spirit* draws them. So, *My* children, put your faith and trust in *Me*, the *Creator* of all things. *I* love all *My* children with an everlasting love and will always make a way.

JULY 26, 2016

For all believers, do not look to the right or to the left or in front or behind you. Look upward, *My* people; your *Savior* draws nigh. Don't look at the horrors about you. Look to the *God* that saved you. Look to *Him* for peace and comfort. Look to the *Lord* in your hour of need. Everything around you may be in shambles, yet look to the *Lord* of your salvation for all your needs. All you see and hear around the world is the enemy working overtime. *He* knows that *His* time is short and getting shorter each day. Believers, pray earnestly for those affected by violence. Pray for those that have committed the acts of violence. Pray that they will seek help and get forgiveness for their crimes against humanity. Pray for those that have lost loved ones through an act of violence. Pray that they will not become bitter but will mourn their losses and seek the comfort from *God Almighty*. Believers, seek *Me* in your hour of need. Just call out *My* name. *I* am here, *My* children!

People of faith, were you watching and listening to all the conversations regarding the choices you will make for the person who will preside over your nation? Be on high alert and sift through all the negativity and look for a grain of spirituality. People declaring they are Christians is only a word to them. The people that say they are Christians will be known by the fruit of the spirit they produce. Their words will line up with *the Word of God*. People professing Christianity and go against the teachings of the Bible cannot call themselves Christians. Christians (real Christians) are follower of the *Lord Jesus Christ* and all *His* teachings of the Bible. False Christians speak blatantly against the true teachings of the Bible. They change the teachings to suit themselves their point of view. Real Christians follow *My* precious *Holy Word* and believe in it, for it is food for their very soul. In regard to the decision-making, you, *My* people, listen to the prompting of the inner voice of *My Holy Spirit* which will lead you and guide you in a quest for the truth. Listen carefully to what is being expressed and then compare it to *the Word* of the living *God*. Many so-called Christians make promises they cannot keep. True followers know that the one true *God* keeps all *His* promises, and *His* words are true and never change to suit one's circumstances. Remain in *Me* and *My Word*, and *I* will remain in you. *I* will never leave nor forsake you. That's *My Word*.

JULY 28, 2016

People of faith, you look around your land and see the horrific acts of violence being committed on mankind. Some will ask where is *God*, and why is *He* allowing this to happen? *I* am here, people of faith, in the midst of all that's going on waiting for *My* creations to call upon *My* name. *My* people, everyone was given a will (a choice). *I* will not come against their will. Some say they are doing the will of *God*. Not true! Others will say they are ridding mankind of evil. Whatever reason in a person's mind, there's no excuse for the tragedies, whether provoked or otherwise against a fellow human being. *My* heart breaks for the ones left behind without their loved ones. Survivors of the tragedies need to be told of a *Heavenly Father* that live, love, and comfort them and always be there in their hour of need. *My* people of faith are always close at hand after a violent act. They are willing to help the victims and families sometimes just by praying for them. Remember, people of faith, *I* am still in control. Sometimes it may not seem as though *I* am, but don't go by looks or circumstances. *I* am in the midst!

JULY 29, 2016

Part 1

People of your nation, most of the violence happening in your nation is a result of retaliation because some individual was wronged one way or another. Mankind should not take the law into their own hands but instead leave it to the people in charge. Taking the law in one's own hands only leads to destruction, violence, and more violence. When will the people turn from their wicked ways and seek *My* face? Then *I* will hear their prayers and forgive their sins and heal their land. One thing remains for the people to see these violent attacks are from the enemy. One way to stop all these violence is to forgive the ones that have wronged you and show the nation you possess love and forgiveness, not hatred. Unforgiveness feeds hatred and leads to violence. People don't give in to any acts contrary to *the Word of God*.

Part 2

To some Christians, there are people who profess they are followers of the *Lord Jesus Christ*. They claim this openly and yet don't follow the teachings in *My Holy Word*. They talk of a different teaching that adheres to mistreating, harming, and hurting others, all in the name of *God*. These teachings are acts of violence. They believe they are cleansing society of the evil in the land. They also are seeking after revenge. If these people would study *My Word* and see that revenge is *Mine*.

JULY 30, 2016

*M*y brethren, in your world, there is a lot of beauty underneath the facade of outward appearances. Look beyond the outer garments to the inner person. *I* believe there is good in all *My* creations. Sometimes the beauty is buried beneath anger, hatred, frustration, and depression. *My* brethren, go forth and exclaim *the Word of God* to all that have ears to hear what *the Word of God* is speaking. *My* people, you can uncover the beauty in those that are suffering by showing them the love of *God* and *His* plan of salvation. When the lost come into *My* kingdom, they will begin to see the world and all its beauty through different eyes. *My* brethren, it's up to you, the chosen ones, to go forth and proclaim the coming of the *Lord*. Proclaim what is in store for those that love the *Lord* and follow after *His* kingdom.

JULY 31, 2016

Today is a good day to praise the *Lord*.
Today is a good day to count your blessings.
Today is a good day for all those who love the *Lord* to say so.
Today is a good day to sing unto the *Lord*.
Today is a good day to rejoice and be glad.
Today is a good day for all believers to come together.
Today is a good day to give thanksgiving.
Today is a good day to honor your *Lord and Savior*.
Today is a good day for many healings and miracles.
Today is a good day for loving the *Lord*.
Our comfort and happiness depends on what we are to *Christ*, not what we are in the world!

AUGUST 1, 2016

Are you servants? You must declare this day whom you will serve. Will you serve your *Lord and Savior*, or the god of your world? You can't serve *God* and mammon because you will love one and hate the other. Upon making the choice to serve the *Lord God* as *Savior*, then servants of the *Almighty*, stand firm on your beliefs. Upon serving your *Lord*, you must go forth into all the nations of the world preaching the good news. There will be trials and tribulations, also temptations. Remain in *Me* and let *My Word* abide in you. When the trials and temptations occur, you need to declare to the enemy that you are covered by the blood of the *Lamb of God*. No weapon formed against you will prosper; by *His* stripes, you are healed. *I* desire all *My* servants to be loyal, honest, and faithful and possess love for all mankind, showing compassion for all those in need by lending a helping hand, helping the elderly by being a witness for *God*, standing firm for all to see that you serve the one true *God*, and *Him* alone you will serve. The choice is yours!

AUGUST 1, 2016

Daughter,

Recently you received a word of knowledge from a sister in the *Lord*. That word was from your *Heavenly Father*. When *I* speak of a friend, *I* think of you, *My* daughter. You rearranged your life and lifestyle to be with a sister in *Christ* in her hour of need. She doesn't have close relatives that were able to stay with her. You, *My* daughter, took the word *friend* to the next level. You gave up all to be at the side of your dear friend. It's *My* desire that all *My* chosen ones would look to you as an example of friendships. You are a blessing for all in whom you encounter. *My* daughter, you are blessed beyond measure. You have chosen not to be recognized for your sacrifice. Stay humble, *My* daughter. You already have your blessing in glory!

Your True Friend,
Jesus

*M*y children, do you glorify *God* before all mankind? Do you speak and sing *His* praises? The *God of Heaven* came to earth to show the lost the only way to eternity. *He* walked among the people, healing all their diseases. *He* spoke of many things in regard to salvation and eternity. *He* was persecuted, beaten, denied, and then crucified! Buried and rose on the third day. Now seated at the right hand of *God. He* suffered all these and more so that all mankind could be saved and spend eternity in *Heaven* with *Him.* Now *I* ask again, do you give *God* the glory and honor *He* deserves? Do you speak of *Him* in your daily lives? Are you doing all you can to spread the gospel to all mankind? Do you witness to all that are lost? Do you speak of *His* marvelous and undying love for all *His* creations? Do you tell of the compassion and forgiveness for sins? Now if you are doing all that to spread the good news, then *I* call you *My* chosen ones!

AUGUST 3, 2016

Believers, in your daily lives, are you accepting things that go against the teachings of the Bible? Do you speak out and declare that it is wrong and therefore sin? When you do not speak against sin you see, then you are as much as part of that sin as the sinner. This is a problem in your world. Too many believers are sitting silently by while sin is taking on a new form. It's being shown to you by programs you watch, by the entertainment you see. Also in your daily path, you will come across many types of sin. It's up to you as believers to speak against any known sin. Sin can take on many different forms, but regardless, sin in any form is sin. As believers of *the Word of God*, *My* people, speak out! You will be called names; you will be mocked and persecuted. Stand firm and don't back up or back away. It's up to *My* believers to go to all the nations and teach *the Word of God*. Tell them that sin in any form will not be accepted in the kingdom. *I* love the sinner but not the sin. Show the sinner the plan of salvation.

It's free to all who choose it. Be alert and watchful what goes into your mind and thought life. Accept only good and encouraging ideas, those that will benefit others, being careful to ignore the hurtful things.

*M*y children, seek ye first the kingdom of *God* and *My Holy Presence* in your daily life. Seek *Me* above all else. Put *Me* first in everything in your life. *My* children, do you try to obey *My* teachings? *I* know some will fall because of their humanness. Pick yourselves up and declare that you are a child of the living *God* in whom all blessings flow and a rewarder of those who diligently seek *His* face. *My* children, seek *My* face because *I* am no respecter of persons. Seek *Me* above all else. When you decide to seek *Me* and *My Presence*, be prepared for distractions! They will occur. The enemy is working tirelessly to occupy *My* people to keep them from seeking *Me*. Declare, *My* children, to the enemy that you are a child of *God* covered by the blood of the *Lamb*, and that no distractions will keep you from seeking your *Heavenly Father* and *His* will for your life. Now, *My* children, *I* ask you: "Do you love *Me*?" In answering yes, then go forth and feed *My* sheep. Go into your nation and preach the good news to all the lost of your world.

AUGUST 5, 2016

S aints, *I* call you saints because you follow after *Me* and the teachings. Saints, you will face obstacles in your pathway of life. It's how you deal with these occurrences that make you a saint and a follower. When you or a loved one are diagnosed with a disease or illness, then do what *My Word* declares. Call upon the elders of the church, and in faith, lay hands on the person and pray for a complete healing. Are you having financial problems? *I* am the great problem solver. *I* will call forth the blessings of *Heaven.* Are you feeling alone? In *My Word*, it declares the *I* will never leave you or forsake you! Are you concerned about your children? *My Word* declares to raise them in the way of the *Lord*, and they will not depart from it. Upon following *My Word* and its teachings, *I* declare you are the righteousness of *God*, and *I* call you *My* saints.

AUGUST 6, 2016

My dear children, you have been saved by *My* grace and given the righteousness of *God*. The only thing you have to do is accept it and believe it. It was not given to you by your works. Nothing you could do will earn your salvation. It is *My* free gift to all people that accept *My* plan of salvation. The problem seems that *My* creations choose not to accept it and go about their life doing things on their own. They feel they don't need any help in their situations. Sometimes then upon realizing they don't have all the answers to their problems and don't know what to do, in frustration call upon *Me*. *I* am here patiently for those in need to call out *My* name. Just say, "Help *Me, Jesus*!" That's all it takes, and *I* will be there for anyone seeking *My* help. Just call upon *Me*.

Believers, it's a daily battle between your flesh and the spirit of *God*. You must crucify your flesh daily. Do not let your fleshly desires pull you away and back into the world. Repent daily and seek forgiveness and guidance in your walk with the *Lord*. Take control of your thought life and don't dwell on circumstances you cannot change. Seek *Me* and *My Holy Spirit* for answers to your situations. Trust and depend completely on *Me*, and *I* will show you the solutions to your problems and situation. By you seeking *Me*, that closes the gap and won't let the enemy enter into your thoughts. Trust in *Me*, believers; *I* am just a prayer away.

AUGUST 9, 2016

My chosen ones, look about you; everywhere you turn, sin is there! In everything, some people choose evil over good, not even realizing what they are doing. Sin abounds in material things, the things you see, the things you hear, and in the things you do. Pray, *My* people, before all that you do. Cover yourself with *My* precious blood. Seek *My Holy Spirit* for guidance and leadership. Do not open the door to sin by even a small crack. The enemy will slip in unaware until it's too late. Remind yourself daily that you are a child of *God* and covered by the blood of the *Lamb*. Sin can only have access if you allow it. Put on the armor of *God* and do battle. *I* am sending you into a den of thieves, so be prepared to do warfare continually. Plead the blood over family members daily, covering them with prayer. The devil is like a roaring lion seeking whom he can devour. You are called *My* chosen ones for taking back what the enemy has stolen. You're putting him under your feet where he belongs. Take heed, *My* children. It's an ongoing battle until *I* come again.

AUGUST 11, 2016

To gentile believers, you are among *My* chosen generation. You have been grafted into *My* holy kingdom, set forth to bring the good news to all the lost. As people of faith and believers of *the Word of God*, count it a blessing to be able to witness to the lost souls of the world. *I* have chosen you; you didn't choose *Me*. *My* plans for you is to speak of *My* salvation to all mankind. The accuser of the brethren will do everything he can to interrupt your calling. Set your course, and do not falter, aim straight for the target, which are the souls of the lost. Do not let anything keep you from attaining your goal. The accuser will throw everything at you. *He* will even use family and friends to dissuade you. Do not alter your course. Do not give him a foothold in your life. Seek *My* face and the help of the *Holy Spirit*. *My Spirit* will lead and guide you with your battles of warfare. Lean entirely on the *Spirit of God* and not on your own understanding. Keep your mind and heart focused on the salvation of the sinners of the world.

AUGUST 12, 2016

To all the lost of the world, do you believe in life after death or in eternity? Have you ever been told of either? There is an eternal life after death in your world. You may not know about it or even believe it. That doesn't mean it doesn't exist! Sinners, think about this: Upon your last day on earth, your last hour or minute with death staring you in the face, wouldn't you like to have an eternal life with the *Creator* of all things and to live in the heavenly realm? For the nonbelievers, to them, death is final. When they are buried, that's the end. Nonbelievers, would you rather have an alternative? You see, whether you believe or not, you still, one day, will stand before *God* for final judgement. It's *My* desire for everyone to accept salvation and spend eternity in *Heaven*. *I* love all *My* creations. *I* love them not the sin. When they allow their eyes and ears to be opened, they will see all what's in store for them who choose *Jesus Christ* as *Savior*.

AUGUST 13, 2016

People of the world, why are you seeking satisfaction from all the wrong things in your world? When you become sick, you call upon a physician. Can't you see and understand that I, *God Almighty*, am the great physician? The physicians of your world were given their wisdom and knowledge by *God*. Yet they think that their knowledge comes from their education and experiences. Why can't they see that everything comes from *God the Creator* of the universe? When searching help for finances, they seek a financial advisor instead of seeking the one that hold all the riches of the world in *My* hands. Seek *Me* for all your needs. Seeking comfort after a disaster? Remember, *I* am the great comforter and all the hope they will need. *I* will not leave nor forsake them. People, you need to know that whatever your need in your life, *I* can provide if only you will seek *Me* and *My* plan of salvation. *I* am the great *I* Am.

AUGUST 15, 2016

*M*y beloved children, *I* have sent you into a world darkened with sins of every kind. You should be a glowing light of brightness to all you encounter. Others should look at you and see the love, glory, and presence of your *Heavenly Father*. The words flowing from your mouth should permeate those all around you. Your speech should be as milk and honey. When you walk, you are taking the steps of the *Lord* leading to righteousness. When you reach for someone, these are the arms of the *Lord* reaching to a lost generation. When you help someone in need, you are helping to show others the love of *God*. In talking about the *Lord*, you are planting seeds of salvation. Continue letting your little light shine for all to see and say that you belong to *God*. So press on, *My* children, and glorify your *Father in Heaven* by all you say and do! Don't let anything deter you from your mission to bring the gospel of hope to this sinful world.

AUGUST 16, 2016

To all believers, you must stand firm and be faithful, loyal, and an overcome until the time of *My* coming. Temptations will arise before you. Stand against all the wiles of the enemy. Declare *He* has been defeated and will no longer be able to rule in the lives of you and your family. Declare this daily, hour by hour, minute by minute if necessary. Don't be fooled or persuaded by any of *His* tactics. Do not believe or fall for any of *His* lies. Believers, you must remain strong in the kingdom of *God* and persevere above all else. Only those who remain of faithful until the very end will inherit the kingdom of *God*. Stay in *My Word* and let it be food for thought and soul. When the enemy comes to you with his lies, be able to quote *My* Holy Scriptures. Put on the armor of *God* daily because in this sinful world, you will be doing battle continually from now on until the coming of your *Lord*. Take heed, believers, *I'm* coming back for those who persevere until the end.

*M*y friends, yes, if you have accepted *My* plan of salvation and made *Me* the *Lord* of your life, then *I* call you friend. You can come before *Me* with any problems or any concerns you might have. *I* am readily available. *I* will listen intently to you and give solutions to all your concerns by way of answered prayer. Friends, you don't have to come before *Me* with elaborate prayers; just speak what's in your heart. Just a simple prayer coming from one's own heart is a very meaningful approach. Just be yourself as *I* created you. No fancy speeches, no fancy words, just a simple prayer before the *Lord* who saved you from all your sins. Friends, sometimes you may try to impress others by being someone different. Don't fall into that trap! You are not like others in your world. *I've* called you out of the darkness into *My* marvelous light. You were created in the image of *God*. You are not like any other; remember this! So friend, you see, you have the greatest relationship of all mankind with *God Almighty himself*.

To this chosen generation, do you have enough faith to sustain you? Remember, faith comes by hearing *the Word of God* and then acting upon it. Your faith increases when you put it into action. Upon salvation, you were all given a measure of faith. It's up to you to increase it by hearing and believing *the Word*. Now secondly, *I* ask, do you have enough trust in the *Lord* to sustain you? Do you understand what trust really means and stands for?

Totally
Relying
Upon the
Son of *God*
To fulfill *His* promises

By trusting *Me* to do what *I* say and believing that *I* will do whatsoever *I* say, this will increase your faith and bring you to a closer relationship with *Me*. Take heed, *My* chosen generation, and don't succumb to the wiles of the enemy. Put your faith and trust in the one and only true *God*.

AUGUST 19, 2016

People of faith, do you truly believe in *My Holy Word* and all its teachings, beliefs, promises, and blessings? Do you believe *My Word* is true and everlasting? *The Word of God* is for all believers to live by, be guided by, to be taught by, to be committed to, and to desire all the blessings it promises to be poured out upon all mankind. People of faith, you must love *the Word of God*, read it daily, and let it penetrate every part of your body. Let it soak in like sponge absorbing water. Rid yourself of anything that would keep you from tasting what *I* have for you in *My Word*. *My Holy Word* is not to be taken lightly or literally. It is *the Word of God* spoken through the generations by prophets, apostles, and disciples for all mankind to believe. Some try to change *the Word* to suit their own beliefs. *My Word* is not to be added to or changed in any way. If you do not understand the Scriptures, ask your *Heavenly Father* for spiritual insight.

People of faith, trusting in *Me* means for you to turn everything in your lives over into *My* capable hands. Leave all your problems, all concerns, all sickness, all your cares, and woes to *Me*, your *God* and *Father*. By trusting and believing on *Me* and turning control of your life over to *Me*, you will find peace and understanding, not as the world knows but a heavenly peace. *My* people, you must trust *Me* completely with no reservations or no hesitations. People of faith, *I* will do what *I* say *I* will do. *I* do not change nor does *My Word* change. You can believe *My Holy Word*. It has the answers to all your cares and problems. Here's what trust means:

To   Solely
Relinquish   To the Trinity!
Unbelief

*M*y chosen ones, people, you don't seem to understand the fullness of your position in *My* heavenly kingdom. *My* people, you have been given all the same power that was given to *My Son Jesus*. You can go forth laying hands on the sick for their healing. You have the authority to stand up for your beliefs and your faith in the *Lord Jesus Christ*. You have been blessed with all spiritual blessings when you became a child of *Mine*. It's up to you to go forth and show the love of your *Father*. It's up to you to plant the seeds of salvation. As a chosen generation, it's your privileges to speak about your *Savior* and all the wonderful things *He* is doing and has done in your lives. The time is now for all *My* children and all *My* chosen ones to go forth and be willing to do battle against the enemy. Lost people of the world are dying from lack of knowledge. You, *My* chosen ones, have been given the greatest gift to help bring the message of salvation to all mankind. Now go forth and tell the good news and tell the world of the things yet to come to those who refuse *God's* plan of salvation. Tell them of the horrific things awaiting them after death for those who do not believe. Spread the gospel with love, compassion for all mankind. Those who have ears, let them hear what *the Word of God* is saying to all people.

AUGUST 24, 2016

My dear children, when will you stop trying to please the people of the world? Don't concern yourselves with pleasing them but instead put forth that effort in pleasing *Me*. Don't fret yourselves with the things going on in your world. Just be concerned with your lives and the lives of family members. When situations affect your immediate family and or lifestyle, then it's time to do battle! The rest of the problems, leave to *Me*, and *I* will handle them. Put everything into *My* care. Turn complete control of your life and the lives of all family members over to *Me*. Be not concerned with the world's views. Most are corrupt and go against *the Word of God*; be diligent in *the Word* and in prayer, seeking *Me* in all you do. Be open to the guidance of *My Holy Spirit*.

AUGUST 25, 2016

Christians, there are some among you that are not setting a good example for the lost. Remember, followers of *My Holy Word*, that all the world is watching and waiting for you to fall into sin, allowing them to call the Christians hypocrites. People of the world imply that Christians say one thing and do another. Be careful of the followers of the examples that you are putting forth for others to see. Everyone will be watching how you handle dire situations, how you deal with family matters, how you perceive the happenings all around you. Christians show the lost of the world that your faith and hope is in *Jesus Christ* and *Him* alone. Show how the *Lord* helps you in daily living, by guidance and all over love and compassion. Be the light of the world which you were called to be. Show the lost ones of this world that you are faithful to *God* and in *Him* all blessings flow. Also, you will honor *Him* and *His* kingdom forever. Let them see *Me* in you, *My* children.

AUGUST 26, 2016

My people, it's very difficult living in your world and maintaining your faith while sin abounds everywhere. Staying true to your faith and beliefs is what distinguishes true Christians from those who profess they are Christ followers. Your response to situations all around you determines your relationships with your *Heavenly Father*. *My* people will seek *Me* for all their situations, giving thanks for all the good blessings, being thankful for everything. *My* people can come confidently before *Me* in all situations for help. Sinners of the world try to solve their problems on their own. Eventually getting deeper into the miry clay. It's only then they cry out for help. *My* people, you have been pulled out of the miry clay and set upon a rock. Now go forth shining with a heavenly beam and be a witness for all to see. Remind yourselves that greater is *He* that's in you than he that's in the world. Believers, the whole world is watching closely!

AUGUST 27, 2016

Believers, if *My* people would call upon *My* name, humble themselves and turn from their wicked ways then *I* would hear from *Heaven* and heal their land. These words should be published and posted everywhere. There are many people among the world that has not heard this saying from the Bible. Maybe if more of the people knew about and believed this verse, they would do what it declares. It's going to take all the people that are tired of all the senseless killings, all the earthquakes, all the disasters, all misfortunes, and all acts of violence to be willing to get on their knees and seek salvation and then turn back to *God*. Then *I* will hear from *Heaven* and heal their land. Some don't even see the wrong doings in the world maybe because they personally benefit financially from disasters. One day, they will answer for everything. Pray, *My* people, pray for your nation, world, and the people in it. Pray that they will turn from sin and put *God* back into their lives and nation again.

AUGUST 29, 2016

Followers of the *Lord Jesus Christ*, are you using your spiritual gifts wisely? Do you use them to honor your *Lord and Savior*? They are as the words imply—spiritual gifts. These gifts are given freely to all believers for the use of bringing glory to *God the Father*, *God the Son*, and *God the Holy Spirit*. Use them effortlessly and continuously to benefit churchgoers and people of faith. Your spiritual gifts are to edify the church and the congregation, also to help you as an individual in your prayer life and daily walk with the *Lord*. You can never pray too much in the spirit. Praying in tongues or in the spirit edifies the person. But giving a message at your church in tongues with interpretation edifies all the congregation. The prayer language is not meant for show or to put on display but only to glorify *God Almighty*. *I* speak of the gifts, yet the greatest gift and most important is love. Without love for *God* and others, the spiritual gifts are useless with no meaning. Use your free gifts to bring glory to *God the Father*!

*M*y people, *I* stand at the door of your heart knocking, just waiting to be invited in! If only the lost people of the world could see and understand all the things that are in store for them when they come to know *Me*. Then upon accepting *My* plan of salvation, people will experience love unspeakable, peace, joy, and knowledge that they are a child of *God*. This position is not comparable with anything on the earth. The love *I* have and share with *My* children is greater than any love professed on earth because it is a godly love. Come and experience all that *I* have for all those who are called to *My* glorious kingdom. There will be trials and tribulations because you live in a broken world without any conscience of wrong. In the opinions of the world you live in, others may not understand you when you choose to follow *Me*. They may ridicule you. Take heart; all those who persevere until the end will inherit the kingdom of *God*. Be reminded that above all else, *My* love for *My* chosen ones is eternal. Only those who stay faithful until end will inherit eternity!

AUGUST 31, 2016

Believers, you have been blessed with many spiritual gifts. Use them to benefit others; bring glory to your *Father* and edification of the church. I'm specifically speaking of the prophetic messages in tongues, interpretation, praying in the spirit. They are to be used wisely for profit to all. These specific gifts are not for show or display but to be used for one purpose only—to glorify *God*. In the churches upon a spoken message in tongues, there should be an interpretation. The *Holy Spirit* will not give a message unless someone yields to interpretation because these messages are to edify the body of Christ. *My Holy Spirit* will use any available vessel to bring forth messages. Listen intently to what *the Word of God* is speaking to the congregations in today's world then discern it and line it up with *the Word*. Sometimes even some false prophetic messages can get into your churches. Make a comparison to *My* Scriptures. Take heed and be on the alert so that you won't be deceived.

SEPTEMBER 1, 2016

Saints, are you awaiting the return of your *Lord and Savior*? Are you preparing yourself in this life? Are you doing all you can to increase *My* kingdom? Are you studying *My* precious Holy Scriptures? Are you walking daily in the path *I* put before your daily praising the *Lord*? Are you giving thanks daily to *Him* who save you from your sins? Are you giving tithes and offerings to further *My* kingdom? Are you working to harvest the lives of the lost? Do you give help to all those in need? Do you honor your *Heavenly Father* with words of love and praise? Will you be faithful until the end? Does your mind ponder upon heavenly things? These questions *I* have asked of you are for all *My* saints. These are questions each saint should ask themselves. The answers to these questions should be *yeah* and *amen*! Upon answering yes to all these questions, you are in agreement with *Me* then *I* call you *My* good and faithful servants. Go forth, *My* children, to all the world telling of the goodness of *God*. Say to all that *I* am coming soon, and *My* reward is with *Me* to repay all those who are faithful until the very end.

SEPTEMBER 2, 2016

To all believers, *I* cannot declare this enough for you to be wary and alert to false teachers and false teachings. Consider what is being taught and compare it with *the Word of God*. I'm saying that you, believers, should know the Holy Bible so that when someone is teaching you on any subject pertaining to the Bible, you will be able to discern what's false and what's true. The *Holy Spirit* will quicken you when things don't line up with *the Word*. It's easy for believers to be misled if they aren't reading the Bible. This is why it's imperative to read and study and memorize *the Word of God*. Feed upon it daily, constantly letting the words penetrate your spirit, mind, and soul. As you read and study *the Word*, you will start to realize even reading the same verse that you have read before, it will speak differently to you. Each time you read *the Word*, each time you will get a different meaning and different understanding. *My Word* is meant to encourage you, bring you comfort and joy, to guide you in the pathway of life, and to teach you about your *Heavenly Father*. So *I* say again, beware of those who teach differently than what's contained in *the Word*. Be warned, *My* people, and be on high alert. Remember, the enemy is running around to and fro seeking whom be may devour; *He* will use anything or anyone to draw you away from *Me*. Pray before you read *the Word* and pray for insight to its teachings.

Saints, as you observe and honor Labor Day in your world, remember, it means a day to refrain from labor. *I* say, do not refrain from your labor and of the harvest for the lost souls of the world. They are everywhere you turn, so equip yourselves with the full armor of *God*. Share your testimony of faith and salvation. Remember, they walk among you in your daily lives. Some may even be your loved ones or friends. Share the gospel of grace and saving salvation with all. Plant the seeds of deliverance, hope, love, comfort, and joy. Tell them of the grace of your *Lord*, of *His* mercies, and blessings. Saints, you are laborers in a giant vineyard. Go forth and reap the harvest. Some people may be uncertain about salvation. They may have unanswered questions. That's why, *My* saints, you should be knowledgeable in *the Word* so as to answer their questions. You will have some people who say they have already received salvation, and yet they are doing things contrary to *the Word of God*. You should explain that once you receive salvation, you live in the world but are not of the world because the *Spirit of God* resides in you! These people need to make a new commitment and renewal of their faith to the *Lord*. It's up to the laborers in the vineyard to reap a new harvest for the kingdom.

SEPTEMBER 5, 2016

Saints, are you laborers in the vineyard? Are you sowing seeds to the lost? Saints, pick up your sword and begin to harvest for *God*. The fields are ripe in your world waiting for the harvester. Why, saints, are you lingering, meandering, and wondering which way to go? The harvest is everywhere you turn. They are in front of you, behind you, and on both sides of you. So go forth with diligence, love, and compassion to begin the process of harvesting all whosoever will come into *My* kingdom. Don't be slack or slothful, but be ever faithful because I, the *King* of kings, am coming soon very soon. It's apparent that there are some among you that accept things of the world that are sinful and contrary to *the Word of God*. Even some saints believe that certain sins are permissible. Not true! Sin is sin in any form if it goes against *My Word*. *The Words of God* are for *My* people to live by, not to distract for their own agenda. Go forth, saints, and tell of the goodness of the *Lord* and seek all the lost souls in your world. The time of harvest is now!

SEPTEMBER 6, 2016

Followers of the *Lord Jesus Christ*, sometimes while following *Me*, you will get off course. Don't be alarmed; just call out to *Me*, and *I* will lead you back on your pathway to *Me*. Keep your mind and thoughts set on the heavenly realm. There will be interruptions and sometimes false directions. Do not be fooled! When you follow *Me* closely, *I* mean reading and studying *My Word*; you will see that all fall short of the glory of *God*. You are human and will misstep; it's what you do upon a misstep that defines who you are in Christ. *My* followers know that they can do nothing in their own strength, but with *God*, all things are possible. *My* followers, do not listen to any teachings that go against *the Word of God*. Let those false teachings pass through your thought life without ever taking hold. Only *My* precious *Holy Word* can get a hold into your mind. Dwell upon it; let it soak into your inner being; let it soak into your mind, body, and spirit. Let it overwhelm you. Still, there will be constant distraction and interruptions from the enemy. You, *My* followers, have all the knowledge and equipment to overcome anything the devil can throw at you. You are after all *My* followers, and as *I* did, you will overcome because *My* spirit is within you, and *I* overcome the world!

SEPTEMBER 8, 2016

People of the world, heed these words of warnings! The time is now for all mankind to realize that your world is fast approaching total destruction. People of the world who don't believe in anything or stand for anything, realize this: The day will come soon when all tongues will confess that there is a *God*. *I* will be coming back soon for *My* people of faith. The sins of the world are an abomination unto *Me*. I'm waiting patiently, hoping for more people to accept the plan of salvation. People are so involved in all the happenings around them and the acceptance of them believes there is no hope. If only they would understand *I* hold the future of all mankind in *My* hands. When, oh when, will the sinners realize that there's more to one's life than the daily routine and their daily existence. By not understanding what *I* offer, they are missing so many blessings and a relationship with *God Almighty*. One day, when you people of the world have had enough then turn to *Me*. Come to *Me* all that are burdened and heavily laden, and *I* will give you rest. Heed these warnings!

Brothers and sisters, are you doing the will of your *Father*? Do you show the love of your *Father* to all you meet? Do you tell them about the love and compassion of the *Father* for all mankind? Brothers and sisters, *I* would have you to sing the praises of your *Heavenly Father*. Tell of *His* goodness, mercy, grace, and forgiveness for all. It's not just for some but to all who will accept *Him* as *Lord and Savior*. *My* brothers and sisters, speak of your eternal inheritance, of blessings poured out which nothing can contain. Tell of the marvelous things that your *Father in Heaven* has done for you, like sacrificing *His* only *Son* on the cross for all mankind. Speak of the things yet to come, like wars and rumors of wars. Tell them of the times you are living in now. Of all the wars, earthquakes, all the famine, pestilences, and violence. Yet in the end of time, these things will seem small compared to what is yet to come for those who do not accept *My Father's* plan of salvation. You see, *My* brothers and sisters, how important it is to share *the Word of God* to all and the plan of salvation. *I* will be coming back soon for all *My* people to gather them up into the holy kingdom, waiting patiently for our family reunion in *Heaven*. There we will see each other face to face. Be about our *Father's* business, *My* brothers and sisters.

Believers, are you allowing *Me* to be everything to you? *I* am the potter, and you are the clay. *I've* created you in *My* image. Now allow *Me* to be your provider, your comforter, your friend, your helper, your healer, your problem solver, but most of all, *I* want to be your *Heavenly Father*. *I* want to be the one you come to for answers about anything. *I* want to be the only one you rely upon during your hour of need. *I* will always be there for you at any time. Just call *My* name, "*Father God*, help *Me*!" Too many believers take their problems to get earthly authorities first, and if they don't answer, then they come to *Me*. *I* am a jealous *God*. Come to *Me* first and foremost for everything. *I* hold all the answers for you in *My* hands. Understand this, believers, choose *Me* and *My* kingdom above all else, above anything the earth has to offer. Come unto those who are heavily burdened, and *I* will give you rest. You must make the choice in your mind-set whom you will seek and serve. Seek after the things of *God* and *His* godly kingdom.

My children, do you understand how wide, how deep, how long, and how high is the love *I* have for all *My* children? *I* love you with an everlasting love. Man's words are unable to define this. Anything they don't understand, they dismiss as worthless. If only all the world could understand *My* love for all *My* creations. As with your earthly parents, some of you will bond and listen to their advice. Some children will rebel and go their own way. This is so with *My* children. There are those in total obedience and totally rely on *Me*. Then there are those of *My* children that choose to do things on their own, believing they can accomplish any feat by themselves. Little do they know that without the *Father*, nothing will prosper. Sometimes *My* children get themselves into predicaments and find no way out. *My* children, come to *Me* your problem solver, and *I* will no way cast you aside. It's *My* desire for *My* children to seek *Me* first just concerning choices, and *I* will advise you. It's up to you to decide what to do. *I* gave all *My* creations a will. *I* won't come against any choice they make. Only by seeking *Me* first can bad decisions be avoided. Now, *My* children, *I* ask you, do you love *Me*? Do you honor *Me* before mankind? Do you respect *My* teachings and words of knowledge? Do you give your *Heavenly Father* all the praise, glory, and honor worthy of a *King*? You, *My* children, are created in *My* image. Be aware of this at all time and glorify the *God* of the universe.

SEPTEMBER 14, 2016

*M*y people, as you come to worship *Me* in your churches, leave your inhibitions at home. Come together to worship and praise *Me* in song and dance. Lift up holy hands in submission to your *Heavenly Father*. Glorify *Me* with the praise of your thoughts and singing. Clap your hands in rhythm to the lyrics of songs. Rejoice all ye people and don't be ashamed of the reverence you show your *Father in heaven*. Do not concern yourselves with what others will think. Come and stand in submission for *I* am the lover of your soul. *I* am *He* who created you, and it is *My Holy Spirit* residing in you. Rejoice all ye people before the *God* of the universe. Worship no other for *I* am a jealous *God*. Do not let hindrances of the world keep you from honoring *Me* in song and dance. *I* love it when *My* people come together with words of praise on their lips and joy in their hearts!

*M*y people, be aware of all the evil that has manifested throughout the world. *I* know that *My* people see all the evil, and they should be on their knees doing battle against the enemy. This type of evil can only be overcome by fasting and constant prayer. So, *My* chosen ones, put on your armor and prepare to do battle. It's going to take all Christians to declare a day of battle. In this declaration, all Christians should come together on a certain day, hour, and be in agreement. Then start praying for all the lost for all the nations. Pray for their eyes and ears to be opened, especially their minds opened to receive *God's* plan of salvation. The evil in your land started manifesting faster when *My* name was taken out of everything. People were ridiculed for even speaking *My* name. There will always be evil in the land until the final days. Yet now, it is multiplying ever so fast. People, you are living in the last days. By praying and fasting for the lost souls, you are adding more to the kingdom. Remember, you are living in the world, but you are not of the world. Be in prayer to overcome some of the evil so as to make your world a little better until *I* come back.

SEPTEMBER 16, 2016

My people, arise all ye followers of the *Lord Jesus Christ*; arise *I* say! You have been asleep way too long. Prepare yourselves to do battle for your *King*. Put on your armor by girding your loins with truth, putting on the breastplate of righteousness. Shod your feet with the gospel of peace. Take the shield of faith. Put on the helmet of salvation and take up the sword of the *Spirit* which is *the Word of God*. Behold, your *King* is coming. Go forth into your world and bring in all the lost. You, *My* people, must go forth and proclaim *the Word of the Lord*. The enemy is spreading false doctrines and people are following because they know not the truth. It's up to all believers to proclaim *the Word of God*. Arise from your slumber and take authority over the enemy. Reveal *His* doctrines as false by declaring the true *Word of God*. Show all of what you speak that it lines up with the Bible. *My Word* is true and will never change. Everything will pass away, but *My Word* remains forever. So *I* say arise all ye believers from slumber and go forth. Your *King* is coming very soon!

To all who have ears, let them hear what *the Word of God* is saying to all nations. Come and see that *God* is good. Come and sample *His* deliverance and salvation. Come all ye that are seeking after materialistic things. *I* hold all the riches of the world in *My* hands. Seek after *Me* and the things in *My* kingdom. Those who have eyes, let them see all the violence around them. By themselves, they can do only one thing, and that is to pray. Together with other believers, they can accomplish much. There are those who have hardened their hearts against any belief in *God*. They have let others who have been hurt and disappointed influence their ideas of Christianity. Not all *My* chosen ones signify all Christians. They can't all be perfect. Only one is perfect, and that is *God Almighty*. Others will fall because they are humans with a fleshy body. Those who fall will seek forgiveness and pick themselves up and go on. You see the difference with *My* chosen ones and those who have eyes and yet don't see. *My* people, know whom to seek. People of the world are still waiting for answer to their problems. Listen, people, when someone is hurting and help is available yet they turn away from it the help of *God*, *God* has all the help mankind will ever need, and because of ignorance, they turn away from the best offer of help they will ever find. Come all ye who are hurting. *I* will comfort you. Make *Me* your *Heavenly Father*.

A chosen generation, yes, you, *My* followers, are a chosen people, saved through grace, and you became the righteousness of *God*. You have been redeemed from the curse of the law. You are new creation. You were purchased with a price—the blood of a sacrificial *Lamb*, *My Son*. Behold, people, start spreading the good news. Speak of *My* redemption and salvation to all the lost ones. Tell them how they can become children of the *Most High God* and belong to *God's* family of believers. The world in which they are living in is only temporary and can be gone in an instant. Whereas *My* kingdom will last forever in eternity. Suffering in today's world will not grant you eternal life in *Heaven*. Only the acceptance of *My Son* and *His* plan of salvation will guarantee your eternal destiny. As followers of the *Lord Jesus Christ*, will people inherit the heavenly realm? Go forth, *My* chosen generation, and spread the gospel.

SEPTEMBER 20, 2016

Lost of the world, if only you, the people of the world, could see your dire need for a *Savior*. Sinners, you should realize that there is more to life than what you are experiencing now. Evil has been around since the beginning of creation. Sinners, you are in a continuous circle going round and round and yet getting nowhere. One day, you will come to the end of it all—death. Now understand, there is more to life than what you are living now. There is a better existence, and it's up to you to choose. In an hour of need, you can make the decision to seek a better life, one in which you accept the *Lord* as your *Savior*. It's never too late, lost people, to gain peace, joy, forgiveness, and most of all, eternal life in *Heaven*.

My son and daughters, today, you experienced what all *My* people are required to do—to bring in all the hurting and lost into the kingdom of *God*. There are hurting individuals everywhere. Look about as you walk through this life for those in need of spiritual guidance and prayer. Both of you have requested in prayer to be used for *My* glory. So be it! You be very gracious to a young man seeking deliverance and help. *I* will undoubtly put more in your pathway as you walk with *Me* in this life. Be ye prepared for all circumstances and for all problems that beset the lost. *I* have opened your hearts to receive all who will partake of the goodness of *God*. Be willing any hour of the day or night to accept all that seek you out. I'm counting on you both to show the love and compassion of your *Heavenly Father*.

People of faith, you must hold on until the very end. Do not falter nor waver in your faith and belief. For it is only those who persevere until the end that will inherit the kingdom of *God*. People of faith, you will go through a lot of trials and tribulations meant only to test your faith. You will be an outcast among your own family and friends. Seek *Me* during these trying times by prayer and thanksgiving. *I* will abide with you and comfort you through your times of trial. *I* am but a prayer away, so reach out to *Me* at anytime, anyplace, and *I* will no way cast you aside. Rely on *Me* for all your needs and all your cares. No one loves you as I. Be aware of *My* ever-abiding presence and glorify *Me* with your words of praise. Fill your mind with *the Word*; let *My Holy Spirit* fill you to overflowing. Remember to seek after the things of the heavenly kingdom and not the things of the world. Thus, you will have a firm foundation. Stay in *the Word* and let it become food for your soul. Remember, only those who persevere until the end will be with *Me* in Heaven!

People of faith, do you possess the peace of *God*, or do you fret over everything? *My* peace *I* give to you surpasses all the worldly understanding. First of all, you need to know the place *I* offer to you. Upon becoming a follower of the *Lord Jesus Christ*, you inherit all the blessings and promises that were bestowed to *Me* from *My Father* which is now your *Father* too. Upon acceptance of the plan of salvation, you have been grafted, or another term adopted, into the kingdom of *God* with all the privileges of that position. So you see, people of faith, *I* have given you a measure of faith, and *My* peace *I* give to you. To experience peace requires that you be united with the *Lord* in active faith, believing that *He* is the *Prince of Peace*. Diligently seek after and pray for peace *My* chosen ones. The time is now for all the Christians of all nations to seek after the peace of *God* in their lives, to have a closer relationship with the *Lord God* of the universe. Shalom.

People of the world, *I* hear all your cries for help in your dire situations. *I* hear the moaning and groaning of the pains of life you are going through. *I* see all the disgraceful things you do. *I* see all the sufferings of mankind. *I* see all the idols you use to amuse yourselves. *I* see people's lives being taken all too soon, often for no apparent reason. *I* hear the innocent cries of lives being aborted daily. *I* see *My* creations doing unspeakable deeds to others. *I* watch as *My* creations are rebelling against *Me* and them saying that they were created different. That's wrong belief. They were created in the image of *God* and are masterpieces in the universe. Yet there are those changing themselves to please others. They are becoming a product of humanity and a product of their own doing. *I* see all because *I* am an all-seeing and all-hearing *God*. *I* am waiting for the people who are in distress and crying to call out to the only one true *God*!

SEPTEMBER 30, 2016

Brethren, hear what *the Word of the Lord* is saying to all who believe. Before your lies, the evil is taking over the minds of your loved ones whether it be your children or a family member. It speaks softly and entices all whom will listen. It speaks of ideas contrary to *the Word of God*, saying that *the Word of God* is not true, telling everyone that there is no *God*. This false teaching is being promoted on a daily basis to all who will listen. Your children are being manipulated through the games they play and what their eyes see. They don't even realize that their thought pattern is being transformed into the beliefs of the enemy. Remember, *My* brethren, the thief Satan comes to kill and destroy. *He* uses anyone to complete *His* purpose. Beware of any teaching, saying, or prophecy that goes against *the Word of God*. This is why you, *My* brethren, should be knowledgeable in the precious *Holy Word of God*. Listen, *My* people, to what *the Word of God* is saying to all *His* saints. Behold this day for all believers to take back what the devil has stolen from you and do not let *Him* gain any more ground. Stop *Him* in *His* tracks with the blood of the sacrificial *Lamb*.

OCTOBER 1, 2016

Saints of the *Lord Jesus Christ*, are you showing the same love, forgiveness, and compassion that has been shown you by your *Heavenly Father*? Do you paint a picture of the likeness of *God* your *Savior* to all of who you come in contact with you? You, *My* saints, have been granted grace from the *Father*. Heed *My* examples set before you as you go about your daily routine. Show the love of your *Father* upon meeting or greeting a stranger. Smile and the whole world smiles with you; let the strangers see the essence of a *Holy God* and yet available and waiting for all who seek *Him* and *His* righteousness. Remember, you are the persona of your *Lord Jesus Christ*. Go boldly forth yet speak softly so as not to deter anyone. Speak lovingly of the things of the kingdom. Tell of the *Mighty God* you serve of whom nothing is impossible. You, *My* saints, are the arms reaching out, the *Lord's* hands touching with love, the feet walking to all the lost of your world. Show the love they are desperately seeking.

OCTOBER 3, 2016

*M*y people, *I* cannot emphasize enough that you, *My* chosen ones, don't accept anything that does not line up with *the Word of God*. When you visit other houses of worship, listen intently to the word being taught. If it doesn't conform to the Holy Scriptures, then lay it by the wayside. Do not let it enter into your thought life. Disregard it completely. There are those teachers that are more concerned with pleasing men than pleasing *God*. This is the state of your world now. More and more pastors are ultimately concerned about pleasing the people and not stepping on their feelings. It seems that that's more important than what *God* thinks. These are the people you want to avoid. Preachers and teachers of *the Word* are to be known by the fruit they produce. Their lifestyle should be above reproach. Do they walk the walk, or do they just appear to? Be careful, *My* people, your world is full of deceivers and false teachers. Be on the alert for those who practice to deceive and cause them to pull away from *God*. *My* people, be knowledgeable in *My Word* so as not to be led astray by any false teachings. Be faithful and studious, and you will reap *My* rewards!

OCTOBER 4, 2016

To all saints, you are the righteousness of *God*. You have been redeemed and purchased for a price. It came by the sacrifice of *My* beloved *Son* and *His* shed blood. That price has been paid in full. Saints, go forth and proclaim and profess all that *God* has done and is doing in your lives—how *He* saved you, how *He* healed you, how *He* made you joint heirs with *Him* in glory. Tell of *His* redemptive powers, of *His* unchanging *Word*, of *His* compassionate love for all mankind. Speak of *His* loving kindness and forgiveness for all who seek him. Saints, go forth and proclaim *the Words of the Lord*. Testify of all the things *He* has done in your individual lives. You, *My* saints, you possess all the gifts and powers of *My* beloved *Son*, so it's up to you to use them. Go forth, saints, in the name of the *Lord*. Be bold but not brazen. Do all things with love and compassion as doing unto your *Heavenly Father*. Be blessed!

People of faith, where does your faith come from? Does it depend on *God*, or does it depend on man? All *My* people have been given a measure of faith. You can increase it by doing it in your daily walks and by hearing *the Word of God*. The more you use it, the more it increases. *My* people, you need to be increasing your faith daily by reading *the Word of God* by doing what *the Word* says. Put it to use in all walks of life. Be thankful in all things by prayer and supplication. When things don't go as you planned, give thanks. When you receive a blessing, give thanks. When in need, give thanks saying, "*Lord*, you will supply all *My* needs according to your riches in glory." In all things, give thanks, praise, and glory to your *Father*. In the midnight hour when things seem impossible, give thanks. Even when you feel alone and unloved, give thanks because your *Father* says *I* will never leave nor forsake you. *I* love you with an everlasting love.

OCTOBER 7, 2016

Saints of the *Lord Jesus Christ*, believers, are you continuously in the work of the *Lord*, or are you in a relaxed mode? Serving, witnessing, and working for the *Lord* is a continual effort. It requires your thought life and mind-set to always be about the matters of the kingdom. You, *My* saints, cannot get comfortable in your faith. If you do so, the enemy will slide in and cause disruptions. Do not give *Him* any second or a moment of thought. Keep all your thoughts of the heavenly kind. Keep working on reaching the lost. The harvest is ripe for picking. Some are so hungry for something different in their lives that they are gullible and can easily be swayed by false teachers. It's up to *My* people to spread the good news of the gospel throughout all the nations. The lost are so thirsty that they will believe the lies of the enemy. Believers, go forth with the true *Word of God*. Tell the lost how to drink from an eternal fountain of water and that they will never thirst again. The lost are susceptible to false teachings because the lies of the enemy have been around since the beginning of time. It's up to *My* believers to set the record straight by *the Word of God*. Go forth all you believers; speak what is true and eternal. Tell of the things yet to come for all the lost who do not accept *My* plan of salvation. Tell of the eternal fire of hell for nonbelievers and eternity with *God* for believers.

OCTOBER 8, 2016

To all the chosen generations, you were saved for a price, the sacrifice of the precious *Lamb of God*. You are of royal priesthood and have been granted eternity with *God*. Now do you, *My* chosen ones, want others to enjoy this privilege? Share all your blessings, all your good tidings with the unsaved. Tell them of the *God of Heaven* that knows all, sees all, and hears all. The *God* who is willing to forgive the person of all sins—past, present, and future. Tell them of the everlasting love of *God* and how *He* is always there for *His* people in their need. Tell of *His* divine mercy and grace. Tell of all the miracles *He* has performed. Share with them of how they can spend eternity with the one and only true *God*. *He* is the *Creator* of all living things. The *Creator* of the universe and all that's in it. Lastly, tell them that they can come into the presence of the *Almighty God*. All that's required is belief in *His Son* that *He* died for them on the cross and rose on the third day. With this plan of salvation, they can boldly come into the presence of *God* with their petitions and prayers.

OCTOBER 10, 2016

To all who proclaim *the Word of God*, are you maintaining yourself above reproach? When others in society look at you and your lifestyle, do they see godly character, or do they see you participating in the things of the world? With *the Word of God* as guidance by its teachings, all pastors, preachers, evangelist, priest, clergy, and chaplains should include the *Presence of God* in everything they do for the *Lord*. They are the representatives of *God Almighty* on earth. They should be a shining example and above board on everything, showing and being a prime vision to see while holding a place of honor. As with all positions in public office, all the individuals should be of great respect and honorable above all else. The lost of the world are watching the Christians in church. They are watching all followers for them to fall or commit sin. Also, they are looking for some way to get people of faith to say or do something contrary to *the Word of God*, trying to entrap them. *My* people, be ready for things the enemy will throw at you. Profess *the Word* and live by it always.

OCTOBER 11, 2016

*M*y people, *I* have set before you standards in which to live by. You should honor all pastors that bring forth *the Word of God* and all its teachings. Honor them with words of praise. If needed, help them financially. The congregation should help the pastors in every venue of their pastoring. *My* people, you should also honor the elderly and the widows of your congregation in their times of needs, whether it be finances or be someone to do chores and or errands for them. In your world today, it is very easy to check on the elderly. Call upon them. Ask if they need prayer. Make yourselves available. Also in your houses of worship, there are things you can help do to further the kingdom of *God*. All *My* people should work together using their *God*-given talents or gifts to help with the missions of saving the lost. It takes all Christian people regardless of faith to work together and seek the lost. As long as an individual believes that *Jesus* died and rose again, then they are born-again believers. *I* desire that those born again work together to further the kingdom of *God*, no matter the faith. There should be no animosity amongst believers. Once making *Jesus* their *Lord*, they are *My* people. Stand together and fight for *God*. United you stand; divided you fall. *I* am with you always!

Christians, there are some amongst *My* believers who profess *the Word of God* and yet don't reflect it. They don't absorb it truly into their spirit being. It's imperative that all Christians try to live godly lives in this corrupted world. Show the love to others as *I* have shown you. Believers, let your spirit and intellect soak up *My* precious *Word* like a sponge. Let it penetrate every fiber of your mind and body. This is what it will take in this sinful world today as sin is more prevalent than any time before. People are flaunting their sins and making a mockery of everything that is sacred and holy. They have no regrets. One day, every knee will bow, and every tongue will confess that *Jesus* is *Lord* of all. Until that day which is fast approaching, be vigilant and faithful in *My* given *Word. My Word* is a help in all your living. It is guidance for anything that may come against you. It reveals the gifts of blessings, promises, and prosperity for all whom will follow after *Me.* Christians, practice and live what you believe. Be an example of your *Father* in *Heaven* who is watching all *His* children.

OCTOBER 13, 2016

Believers, have you ever pondered why the lost won't receive salvation and have rejected *My Word*? The unbelievers have gotten so egotistical even to the point of being all self-sufficient, beginning to believe that they need no one. They believe that they and they alone can do everything in and by their own strength. Little do they realize that even their entire being is from *God*. *I* created all mankind even if they don't believe or if they don't understand it. The lost are so indoctrinated by the things of the world. It's hard for them to see beyond their daily life. One day, every person meets death! All believers will be welcomed into the kingdom of *Heaven*. When we pass from this present life, scripture says, "Absent from the body, present with the *Lord*." The lost will have eternity in hell with no chance at repentance. The lost need to make a decision before death as to where they will spend eternity. Once death has come upon you, there is no more chance of redemption. *My* desire is for all to be saved and come into the kingdom of *God*. *I* love all *My* creations and so want them to accept the plan of salvation. *My* beloved *Son* died so that all might be saved. *I* say come!

Son, *I* say son because *I* created you in *My* image. Although you have not accepted *My* plan of salvation, *I* still know you. You have lost your earthly dad! *I* want to be your eternal *Dad*, one you can come to in the midnight hour, a friend you can come to in any situation. *I* will never leave you nor forsake you. *I* am available twenty-four hours a day. All you have to do is accept that *My* beloved *Son* died for you and rose and now resides in *Heaven*. Believe this in your heart, and you shall be saved, belonging then to the kingdom of *God*. *I* love you, *My* son, with an everlasting love. No other can ever love you as I. *I* know your every thought. *I* hear and see all. Deep inside, you are very loving and faithful, also loyal. Why not apply these traits to serving the *God* of the universe? *My* son, the time is growing shorter before *My* coming again for *My* people. Are you going to be counted among them? *I* say again, come to all that are lost seeking refuge, love, and forgiveness. *I* am like a hen gathering her chicks under her wings for protection. *I* want to gather all the lost of the world to bring them to the kingdom of *God*!

OCTOBER 14, 2016

Believers, *My* people, you say you believe and are believers, yet you get so involved in all the worldly happenings around you then forget who is still in control! *I* have not stepped aside, nor have *I* allowed others to reign and rule. I, *God Almighty*, am still in control. Look to no other for answers. When people seek out others in regard for answers, when people seek out others in regard to their problems and concerns, then they are saying that their faith is in man, not *God*. *I* have the solutions for all *My* people's cares and concerns. Look to *Me* in prayer for the situation that's going on in your nation. It looks hopeless for *My* people, but out of hopelessness, *I* can bring joy, peace, and unity. Instead now, you are facing diversity, anger, and confusion. The more you as believers try to solve the dilemma, the more involved and divided it becomes. Why not as people of faith spend quality time in prayer for your nation and all critical situations? You, *My* believers, together can move mountains. In the days and weeks ahead, people of faith, be in constant prayer for who will govern your nation. *I* know sometimes it seems as though there are no *God*-fearing people left. Some are cautious about speaking up for the godly words of wisdom. Believers, do not sit back any longer and allow the ungodly to walk on your beliefs. Stand up for *the Word of God*. Be *God* pleasers, not man pleasers. Pray for all decisions being made. Remember, above all else, *I Am* that *I Am*!

OCTOBER 15, 2016

*M*y children, *I* hear your cries for wisdom and guidance. *I* hear your prayers of concern and for understanding. Listen, *My* children, to *the Words* of your *Heavenly Father*. Ponder all the teachings *I* have put before you in *My Holy Word*. Meditate on them daily, letting them penetrate into your innermost being. Listen intently to what *My* words are saying and speaking to your spirit. All the answers you seek are in the Holy Scriptures. Sometimes it takes a lot of reading and research to fully understand what *the Word of God* is saying. Do not rely on others for interpretation of *My* Scriptures because it will be their own opinion. You yourself get into *the Word* and stay for guidance from *My Holy Spirit* living inside of you. By listening to others, you would be accepting their rendition. Rely on your own understanding because you and you only will answer for your decisions. Upon reading *My Word*, take every thought captive and don't let others sway you. All decisions should be made with a lot of prayer and seeking *My Word*. Your answers are there abiding in them.

OCTOBER 17, 2016

*M*y people, are you prepared to meet the *Lord* when *He* returns? Are you getting ready to receive your crown of glory? *My* coming again can come in the twinkling of an eye. If you haven't lived your life for your *Savior*, then you will receive your just reward. Lost of the world, don't wait saying, "Maybe tomorrow *I* will repent and change." Not tomorrow, people, the time is now before it's too late. People, you don't have to change. Come as you are to the *Lord Jesus Christ*. Seek *His* forgiveness before it's too late. You are not guaranteed tomorrow or what it will bring. The only promise and/or guarantee are found in *My Word*. It states that by accepting the plan of salvation, you are guaranteed entrance into *Heavenly Father*. Why, oh why, do you linger in your doubt? Seek *Me* and the plans *I* have for all who will call upon *My* name! The time is fast approaching for all who will to come unto *My* salvation. *I* am patiently waiting for all who will come. One day, it will be too late. People, don't put off tomorrow what you can do today. *I* am here, *My* people. The decision is yours! Just say yes! Yes! Yes!

OCTOBER 18, 2016

To the lost people of all nations, some of you have a problem believing there's a *God* who created all things. Yes, as you look about the world you live in and see the birds, clouds, trees, and the sky every day and not understand creation, even the air you breathe is a gift from the *Creator*! People, whether they believe or not, have been given their knowledge and abilities from *God*. Most don't acknowledge their talents have been given to them. They accept the credit themselves assuming they earned and worked for their positions. Look, people, if only you would look in *the Word of God* and understand that in the beginning *God* created all living things. *He* created all mankind, giving those talents to help others, like doctors, professors, teachers, preachers, and business owners. Only born-again believers give *God* the glory for all *He* has done in their lives when people awaken to the fact that *God* is the author of all knowledge and wisdom. That in *His* love for mankind and desiring a relationship with them sacrificed *His* beloved *Son*.

P eople of the world, believers are anxiously awaiting the second coming of their *Lord and Savior Jesus Christ*! They have the promise of spending eternity in *Heaven* with *God* when they have accepted *His* plan of salvation. Nonbelievers, those who are lost, only have to look forward to a daily routine. It entails all the problems the world of sin throws at them. Most climb the ladder of business and reach the top and still are unhappy. Many go through each day with dread and no hope for anything better. In their hours of desperation, they seek alternatives to relieve boredom and frustrations. Some even turn to violence to alleviate their pain of hopelessness. So you see, believers, how imperative it is for you to pass on the love and knowledge of your *Savior*. Some will listen, and others will harden their hearts. *My* people, your world is in turmoil and getting worse. What your world doesn't know is their need of a *Savior*. People of the world are getting tired of the way things are happening. They are looking for a change. The only hope for a lost and loosing nation is to call upon the name of the *Lord Jesus*. In *Him* and *Him* alone is redemption for all the lost souls and hope for a nation deep in sin. People of faith, reach out to all who are lost, sharing the blessed hope of salvation. Lost of the world, your only hope is in *God* who sent *His* only *Son* to redeem all mankind. Don't let *His* death and resurrection be for naught. Listen, people, to *the Word of the Lord*.

OCTOBER 20, 2016

Children of the *Most High*, don't bury your heads in the sand when events beset you. Nothing in your world will ever seem right until the people of the world awaken from their sleep, realizing that they have allowed the enemy to take their *God*-given rights away from them. In your laws of government, it stipulates that an individual has the right to worship wherever they please. Yet people of faith are being persecuted because they stand up for their Christian beliefs. *My* people are to obey all man-made laws unless they are in conflict with Bible teachings. Then they stand by what the *Holy Word* says. Don't be confused by all the commotion of lies and deceit. Listen intently to things being spoken and sort out the good intentions. Pray for all in authority, especially those whose decision-making will influence your *God*-given rights. Be in fervent prayer for all those who will govern over you. Do not slack up in your prayer for these individuals seeking positions of leadership. Seek *My* face in all matters that concern you. *I* am waiting for the people to turn from their wicked ways and repent and turn to *Me*. Upon which, *I* will hear from *Heaven* and heal their land. Oh, people of the nations, if they could only see themselves living in sin to see how sin abides in all their lives one way or another. One day, *I* hope very soon *My* people will declare "Enough is enough" and start to take back what the devil has stolen from them and that the sinners will turn from their evil ways!

OCTOBER 22, 2016

My children, no matter what this sinful world throws at you, rejoice! In all things, give thanks with a grateful heart. Whatever happens in your life, rejoice. *My* children, you have the most wonderful gift of all mankind. It's salvation purchased by *My* beloved *Son*. So again, *I* say rejoice! When others in your world are running to and fro yet not going anywhere, you, *My* chosen ones, know where you are going. You are *Heaven* bound when leaving this earth. So rejoice! *I* say rejoice and praise the *Lord* in all things. Look to *Me* for all your questions and answers to prayer. *I* hold the whole world in *My* hands. Rejoice, rejoice, and rejoice that you are children of the *Most High God. I* long to have an intimate relationship with all *My* children. *I* desire for them to talk with *Me* about all things. Come, *My* children, talk with *Me*; spend time with *Me*. Let *Me* show you the love of a true friend, companion, *Father, Comforter*, problem solver, all around everything you will ever need in your world. So *I* say rejoice and be glad who you are in *Christ*.

Warriors, are you preparing yourselves for battle? The times you are living in requires for all *My* people to be clothed in the full armor of *God*, battle armor! The times for many are uncertain not knowing which way to turn. For some, it's a way of life, the only life they know. For others, they are searching for a better life. They are looking in all wrong places for the peace and solace they desire. If only they would turn their eyes heavenward. *My* warriors, you need to start doing battle, coming against all forces of evil. Bind them and declare by the blood of the *Lamb* that they will no longer have a hold on *My* people. Take the authority *I* have given you to defeat the enemy. Pray for people of all nations and come against the evil among you. Those that don't know where to turn, point them in the direction of an eternal *Savior*. Tell them that it is the direction they should go and follow the plan of salvation. It's for all seeking after peace, joy, love, and forgiveness for all who come. Explain to them about the putting on of armor so as to defeat all the fiery darts the enemy will throw at them. Go forth, *My* warriors, the battle is on, and it's a too fierce war designed to cause *My* people to falter. Don't be swayed by the likes of the enemy. Hold on to the truth, *My Word*. Don't let your armor grow weak! Replenish it daily by reading the Holy Scriptures.

OCTOBER 24, 2016

People of faith, you should seek out other believers and other people of faith for your gatherings and meetings. Getting together with other believers will help to strengthen one another and encourage each other in faith. If *My* people withdraw from other Christians, they will eventually grow weaker. So, *My* people, gather together every chance you get and share *the Word of God* with others of faith. Spend time with other Christians with discussions of your faith and beliefs. Share your blessings with others. Confess your concerns and problems, seeking answers by prayer with fellow believers. Together, people of faith, you can move mountains. Continue to have meetings, gatherings, Bible studies to learn and fellowship. Get more involved in *My Word* because the time is coming that all *My* believers will be persecuted for their faith. In your world today, Christians are being abused, threatened, hated, and even killed because of their faith. Great is the reward for those who remain faithful until the end.

OCTOBER 25, 2016

People of faith, hold on to your faith no matter what prevails. Do not let the enemy get a foothold in your thoughts. Stay faithful in *the Word* and obedient to its sayings. Pray to increase your faith. *My* followers must endure many things because of their faith and beliefs. Faith is a precious commodity and increases each time it is used. The more you use it, the more it grows. *My* people, believe for the things unseen. Seek *Me* in all phases of your life. Don't let the sayings of others detract you from holding to what is pure and true. Mankind will stay and do anything for their purpose. It's up to *My* people of faith to be in vigilant prayer for those who practice to deceive. Hold on, people of faith, for the *God* of the universe is still in control. Sometimes it may seem otherwise; don't let that deter you from seeking the truth and holding on to your faith.

OCTOBER 26, 2016

*M*y sons and daughters, if you have been called out of darkness into *My* marvelous light and have accepted *My* plan of salvation, then you are *My* children. Many of you have suffered because of your belonging to the kingdom of *God*. Many have suffered and will suffer because they are being disciplined. *I* will correct all *My* children so they will stay on the right path *I* have chosen for them. Sometimes correction or discipline are necessary for the good of all *My* children. If you have not or do not endure the corrections or discipline, then you are not children of *God*. As with your earthly fathers who discipline their offering, *I* your *Heavenly Father* will correct those who drift from the pathway laid before them. Some will accept *My* reapproval, yet while others will whine and reject it. *My* discipline is because of *My* love for all *My* children to keep them on the right pathway to *Heaven*.

OCTOBER 27, 2016

To all faithful servants, you have all been given diversity of gifts meant to be used for the ushering in of all the lost souls of the world. Use them wisely and with love and understanding, compassion for all equally. Treat all *My* creations with respect and dignity as with one of honor. The gifts and talents you, *My* servants, possess were given to you to help in the multiplying of the heavenly body. Many of *My* servants are able to teach others the precious words of *God*. Yet some use their abilities to serve the needs of other Christians. Some possess the wisdom of a *God*-given ability to understand what is written and can interrupt their meanings. There are those who know how to acquire and collect finances to use to further the kingdom. Then you have individuals who are in constant prayer and intercession for others. You see, all *My* chosen ones have different gifts and talents given by *God* enabled by the *Holy Spirit* for use of gathering all the lost.

OCTOBER 28, 2016

People of faith, are your spirits fed by *the Word of God* or by all you watch and listen to? What you feed your spirit man is what will proceed from your mouth. If you feed upon *the Word of God* and *His* abundant love, then that's what will flow forth from your mouth. Be careful, *My* people, in this day and age with everything around you prompting sinful pleasures and speaking harshly against another person. Don't let yourselves be drawn into the realm of sinful thoughts. Let your words be *yeah* and *amen*. Be ye not only hearers of *My Word* but also doers of it. Do not let temptation creep into your thoughts. Maintain words of *God* and words of worship in your mind and in your spirit. Do not get involved in disagreements with other believers. It causes dissension and hurt feelings. Stay true to *My Word*.

OCTOBER 29, 2016

Christians everywhere, heed this word of warning! The *Son of God* can return at any time. *He* will come without warning in the blink of an eye. Are you, *My* chosen ones, prepared to meet your *Savior*? Are your garments white as snow? Are you clothed with the righteousness of *God*? Christians, tune your ears to the sounds of *God*. Christians tune your ears to the sounds of sin flourishing. Your eyes can see the lost souls all around, and yet you make no attempt to speak to them about salvation. The time has come for all believers to say so. Believers of the *Lord Jesus Christ*, take a stand and speak against the sins of the world. The sinners don't see their sin until it's too late. To them it's a routine or way of life with no hope. They need to know there's more to living than what they are experiencing now. Take the time and effort, *My* followers, and share your faith with all who will listen. Some will turn a deaf ear while others will honor you by being polite. Regardless, plant your seeds to all mankind. It's to their benefit to listen and heed!

OCTOBER 31, 2016

Christians, today is a day the *Lord* has made; rejoice in it. Today is not different than all the others except to some. They use this day continuing to honor evil in the world. All things materialistic, whether it is visual, audio, or spirits which are not from *God* are idols. They are sent to distract people away from *God*. This is even true to some Christians who participate in the traditions of the world. *My* people, you live in the world, but you are not of the world. You are separate from them because of your beliefs. Those that follow after the traditions are also worldly and don't know *the Word*. People of the world will use anything or anyone even little children to lure others into going along with traditions that have been honored many years. Even some of *My* followers deem it all right to go with the flow instead of taking a stand against the evil. The enemy is very sly and will use anything to mislead *My* people as *He* did long ago in the Garden of Eden. Be on the alert to all the tricks of the enemy.

NOVEMBER 2, 2016

Saints, *I* died once for all your sins, past, present, and future. There is no more sacrifice of blood to cover your sins. All it takes is for *My* saints to ask for forgiveness when they sin and believe that they receive it. *I* desire all of *My* saints to seek forgiveness for all known or unknown sins. I've paid the ultimate price. All you need to do is ask, and *I* will forgive and remember them no more. Saints, it's hard in your world of corruption not to sin, whether it be in thoughts or by desire. Do not give into the things the enemy uses to draw *My* people away from *Me.* Be ye loyal in *My Word* and all its teachings. Its guidance will help you handle daily life situations. The *Holy Word* can uplift you, encourage you, save you, and make you a child of the *Most High God.* Trust you read it and let it reside in your spirit, body, and soul!

November 3, 2016

*M*y people, *I've* heard your cries for help and your request for healing. Yet, *My* people, you seem to have forgotten that your healing was paid for on the cross. Sometimes the manifestation takes time. Each person should examine themselves for unknown and known sins in their lives. This can hinder healing. Seek forgiveness, and if you have problems with *My* Christian brothers or sisters, make the effort to right any wrong or misunderstanding. Now in your need of healing, first seek the elders of your church and have them to pray and anoint you with oil. Start believing you receive your healing. Stand on the belief of your healing and don't falter one iota. Just remain faithful and believe you receive the healing that enforces it. Also watch what you say. You can undo any healing with words that are full of unbelief.

Followers of the *Lord Jesus Christ*, wives, are you an example for all to admire, or are you too wrapped up with worldly possessions and desires? It's *My* desire for wives to be in submission to their husbands as husbands are in submission to *God*. This is not intended for wives to be a prisoner or slave but to consult with your husband in all decision-making. Husbands, you are to treat your wives with respect and honor because she is your helpmate. Honor each other with dignity and reverence as unto *Jesus*. In your world, there are women in the role of head of a household. They may have to assume this role through divorce or widowhood. In these circumstances, the women need to look to *Jesus Christ* as their head of authority. *He* will be a substitute for the lost soul mate. Just lean on *Jesus* in any time of need. *My* people, *I* will be your husband, friend, companion, provider, and *I* will supply all your needs. Just come to *Me*!

NOVEMBER 5, 2016

Christians, in these times of corruption and sin in the world, it's imperative for all Christians to remain faithful and true to *the Word of God*. No matter what the circumstances going on all around you, stay true to the *Holy Word of God* in all decision-making. People of faith, stand together praying and believing for the righteous to prevail. It's only through faith and prayers of all *My* people that the enemy will be disarmed and shown as they really are. Constant belittling of others is not what *I* would have *My* people participate in. It's *My* desire that all Christians will humble themselves before *God* and seek *His* response in all matters of your world. Individuals who want to govern others should seek after the will of *God* and the people to be able to successfully do a job right. Praying people will accomplish much!

Heirs to the kingdom of *God*, you have been given many blessings to which you are to share with others in their time of need. Woe to those out of greed that will not contribute to the aid of a brother or sister. Share all that you have whether it be material things or edible items. Also share *the Word of God*. Remember, *My* people, it's better to give than to receive. Everything you possess is a gift from your *Heavenly Father*. By sharing your possessions, you are sharing your love of *God*. Be wise in all you do. Always go one step further than required. Bless all with your blessings from *God*, and reap the heavenly rewards. Holding on to what you have means you don't believe that *I* will do what *I* said *I* would do. In *My Holy Word*, it says that *I* will supply all your needs according to *My* riches in glory. Give from the abundance of your harvest. Give and it will be given unto you shaken up and pressed down. Honor your *Heavenly Father* by giving!

NOVEMBER 9, 2016

Christians, remember, *I* am still in control! Sometimes the prayers you prayed were not answered as you requested. *I* remind you that *My* ways are not man's ways. Stay faithful to your trust and beliefs always by honoring your *Lord and Savior*. Be mindful of your surroundings and the happenings all around you. Just remember, your *Heavenly Father* controls the universe, so pray daily for godly wisdom for all in authority. Pray for all the lost to turn from their wicked ways and seek forgiveness. Then *I* will hear from *Heaven* and heal their land. People of faith, do not stop praying, praising, or worshipping your *Lord*. Stay in continual obedience to *the Word of God*. Seek after wisdom and knowledge so you will be able to help those in need during any situation. Pray. Pray in any time of need.

*M*y people, do you love *Me*? Do you really love *Me*? Do you truly, without a doubt, love *Me* above all others? If you cannot answer yes to all three of these questions, then you need to examine yourselves internally. Check your responses about helping others in need, about loving your neighbor as yourself, about honoring your *Heavenly Father* with words of praise and worship, not just lip service only but action. *My* people, can others see the love of *Jesus* in you, or do they say that that person is worldly? Be loyal to *My Word* and practice what you've learned. When you say "*I* love all mankind," then be prepared to show this love with action. When the world around seems to be crumbling, hang on to the little crumbs and keep praising the *Lord* for *His* blessings and thank *Him* that even in times of woe, *He* is still in control.

My people, sin abounds in your world, but *My* grace is sufficient for all maladies. Grace being the answer for sin in their lives, you wonder why more people don't accept it. It's the procedure of accepting the salvation of *My* beloved *Son* and what *He* accomplished on the cross. Some don't want to let anyone be in control of their lives. They are reluctant to let others make decisions for them. People of the world don't understand what grace is. It is freely given with no strings attached. *My* grace is sufficient to cover and forgive all their sins. By turning their lives over to *Me*, they are saying, "*I* can't do this alone. *I* need help!" *I* am here to guide the people with love, compassion, forgiveness, and understanding. All *I* request in retrospect is honor, loyalty, respect, and most of all, love. *My* desire is for all people to love one another as *I* have loved you. *I* have an everlasting love for all mankind. If they would only hear what the *Spirit of the Lord* is saying. Why do people turn a deaf ear to *the Words of God*?

NOVEMBER 16, 2016

To all houses of worships, are you preparing your people for the second coming of the *Lord*? Do you even believe that one day *He* will return to take *His* people home to be with *Him* in glory? Are you, as leaders or shepherds of your flock, teaching about the coming of your *Lord* and the rapture? Study *My Word*, and it will show you and speak of the coming of *Jesus* for *His* spotless bride (the church). Pastors, preachers, and priests, all heads of houses of worship, it's up to you as leaders in authority to teach biblical truths to get ready your people for the day of the coming of the *Lord*. Prepare your followers and your flock. The *Lord* is coming back for a bride (church) without spot or wrinkle. Speak to your congregation of the things yet to come in the last days. Help them to search themselves and others for sin in their lives. Get it out and don't allow it to persist. Prepare yourselves for the day of the *Lord* is coming for *His* chosen ones. Most of all, *My* people perish for lack of knowledge. It's up to *My* pastors, preachers, and priests to bring *the Word* to *His* people. Then it's up to the people to search and research *the Word* for its understanding and meaning. Christians, *I* am coming soon. Be ye prepared for your *Lord Jesus Christ*, your bridegroom.

NOVEMBER 17, 2016

Saints, are you remaining faithful even through trials and tribulations? Stand firm and hold on to your Christian beliefs and values. Rewards are waiting for those who persevere until the end. There will be some among you who will try to teach a different way to salvation than what is in *My Word*. Be on the alert and let *My Holy Spirit* lead and guide you. *He* will guide and encourage you through *My* Holy Scriptures. Hold on to them and don't let others lead you astray. If you don't know *My Word* by it abiding in you, then you can be lead in the wrong direction and can end up in sin, or worse, you could be pulled away from *Me*. Don't allow others to teach you their version of *My Word*. You read and study *My Holy Word*, and *I* through *My Spirit* will enlighten you with understanding. Remember *My Spirit* resides in you, so don't quench the flow of *His* leading and guiding. Go with the flow, the flow of the *Holy Spirit*.

P eople of the nations! Behold, *I* stand at the door knocking. Will you let *Me* into your houses of worship and come and sit with *Me*? With the lost, *I* stand at the door of their heart knocking to come into their lives. Mostly I'm ignored or pushed aside by thoughts of other things. People are so busy with worldly things that they have no need for spiritual things until something drastic occurs. They then remember to call upon *Me*. *I* hear their cries for help, and *I* am always available for them. Why, oh why, can't they seek *Me* before disasters strike? It's *My* desire for all *My* creations to come and accept *My* plan of salvation so that they will be with *Me* in eternity. *I* see all the sins against mankind and the hurting in your world. If only the people of the nations would treat everyone as they themselves want to be treated. This is a universal commandment, one for all to live by in their lives.

*M*y children who are followers of *the Word of God*, seek *Me* first above all else whenever your peace or joy are threatened. *I* am the great protector of all *My* children who put their total trust in *Me*. *I* will always bring about the plans *I* have for all those who diligently seek *My* face. Remain in *Me* and in *My Word*, and do not partner with the ungodly! When you are in their presence, let them see *Me* in you with the peace and joy that *I* have given to those who follow *Me*. The ungodly because they serve the enemy, the father of lies will undoubtedly use any means to distract *My* children from their first love. The enemy will use everything to unsettle your beliefs and cause doubt. *My* children, *I* will take care of situations that concern you or bring you grief. Just leave all grievances to *Me* your *Heavenly Father*. *I* am in the midst of all your encounters with the enemy. Pray diligently for all loved ones to come to repentance and seek after forgiveness which has to come from the heart. Upon this request, then *My* followers will welcome them into the kingdom.

C ome, one and all to the waiting arms of your *Redeemer*. Behold, *I* stand waiting patiently. Come. To all who have ears, let them hear what *My Word* is saying. *I* welcome all who will come and accept *My* love and forgiveness. One day, *My* wrath will be poured out on all nonbelievers. People, by accepting *My* invitation, you will be saved from this impending disaster at the end of time. Take heed, people that are lost. One day, you will stand before the throne of judgment and give an account of your life on earth. Are you prepared to answer for your lifestyle? Are there things you need to change? Come unto *Me*, and *I* will forgive you of all your sins and wash your garments white as snow! Your sins will be remembered no more. They will be in the sea of forgetfulness. Nonbelievers need to endure a lot and get to the point so disheartening that there is no way out. When they get so downtrodden with no hope, it's then they will realize the need for a *Savior*. *I* will be waiting with outstretched arms. Welcome to all who are lost.

To all believers, come into *My Presence* with thanksgiving in your hearts. Come into *My Presence* with praise. *I* have bestowed many blessings upon all believers. Yet some are not aware of the most precious gift that *I* have bestowed on them. Believers, be grateful for even the smallest blessing. For some, just rising from bed is a blessing for another day. Being able to walk in itself is a blessing. You see, there are some without limbs. Be grateful for what you have. Be thankful if you have a shelter to reside in. There are those living on the streets in your cities. Appreciate the food you eat; may it be a comfort to your body. Many around the world go to sleep hungry. Be grateful that you can worship in your churches of your choice. Some individuals in the world cannot do so without retribution. Be thankful for family and friends; they are a gift from *God*. Be blessed, believers!

NOVEMBER 25, 2016

Christians, this is the season for thankfulness, being grateful for all your blessings from the *Creator*. Acknowledge all of your bountifulness for all to see and hear. Be gracious to all who may be in need, whether it be food, clothing, finances, or any assistance. All *My* people are blessed because they are followers of the *Lord Jesus Christ*. They are blessed because they have been spared an eternity in the lake of fire. It's a blessing for *My* people to belong to the kingdom of *God*. There are more blessings available to *My* followers. All they need to do is start asking and seeking. People of this generation are so blessed with their hearts' desires, and yet they forget to be thankful. Be gracious in all you do for others, and don't forget where your blessings are coming from. Be cheerful and especially thankful for all things big or small in your lives. Be a thankful generation!

NOVEMBER 26, 2016

My people of all nations, be grateful because your *Redeemer* lives. *He* will reside in all who accept *Him* as *Savior*. Be thankful for all things! Count your blessings one by one, giving thanks for each and everyone. Explain from *the Word* of the *Lord* and *His* redemption of all the lost. Spread the gospel to all inhabitants of the earth. Exclaim the *Redeemer* still lives and is waiting for those who will seek after him. *He* has redeemed all from the curse of the law. This, *My* people, should be ecstatic and want to tell everyone of the great and mighty works of the *Lord* on the cross. Being thankful in the season is most pleasing to the *Lord*. Thankfulness at any time is what the *Lord* desires of all *His* redeemed. Gratitude is a very healthful response to all the woes and distress. Thankfulness is a salve for your maladies.

To all believers, your *King* is coming, coming very soon for *His* chosen ones. Believers, listen to these words of warning. There will be great prophets, great teachers claiming a word from the *Lord*. Analyze these saying and words and compare them to the Holy Scriptures. These will be individuals who claim many things, even great miracles. Just remember the enemy can blind the eyes so that people will believe him. *He* will profess many falsehoods because he is the *Father* of them. Believers, let *My* indwelling precious *Holy Spirit* guide you to all truths. Listen to that little inner voice for confirmation. Be alert in regard to all you hear and see. The enemy can sneak a phrase or a picture into something you may deem innocent. If that picture or phrase takes hold, then *He* will multiply it and keep up the barrage until *He* pulls you away from serving your *Lord and Savior*. Be careful with what your eyes see and what you hear. Only maintain the good in your spirit. Take heed, *My* believers, and be even watchful for your *King* is coming!

NOVEMBER 29, 2016

*M*y people, there are so many misconceptions, dissertations, and wrong interpretations of the Holy Bible. Because of the many wrong teachings, some will follow after the lies of the enemy. *My Word* is true and tells each individual how to live, love, and how to be happy and also how to get the peace of *God* in their lives, how to treat others, how to use and enjoy your *God*-given talents and gifts. If you listen to all the lies of the enemy, *He* will tell you that you can do what pleases you no matter who it hurts. One of his lies says to enjoy life to the fullest with no consideration for others. *My* people, these are untruths of the devil himself. Do not be misguided by him. If you want the one true *Word* for happiness, joy, peace, and prosperity, you will find it in *the Word of God*. It's called salvation when you receive the love of *God* which brings peace, joy, and compassion for fellow human beings. People, do not be misled by false teachings. If in doubt, go to *My* Holy Scriptures. Your answers are there for you to read and to live by. Be blessed all who read *My Word*.

November 30, 2016

People of the nations, it seems that there are some among *My* creations that don't believe that the enemy (that old serpent) is real. They believe all the evil of the world is man's doing. True, but that sly devil can put evil thoughts in your mind and see how you react to them. All the evil in the world comes from the enemy—Satan. *His* little cohorts walk around seeking whom they can devour. They take their orders from Satan himself. If he keeps the people worried, confused, and helpless, then they are susceptible to his bidding. All the evil comes from the devil, regardless of what it may be. Sometimes it may come as sickness, poverty, depression, diseases; anything that can cause distress is from the evil one. Remember that only *God Almighty* possesses the good of everything. *God* is good all the time, and all the time, *God* is good. Believe it when *I* say the old enemy is real following *His* evil plans. Take heart, people of the nations, *I* have overcome the world. The devil was defeated on the cross at Calvary. *He* knows *His* time is short. That is why *He* is working overtime to cause people to be in such turmoil. If only people would realize that the evil in their lives is from Satan. *He* is real!

DECEMBER 1, 2016

Christians, are you allowing the enemy into your home inadvertently? Be made aware of all the materialistic items that come into your dwelling place. They may be gifts from individuals who are unaware that these items have satanic overtones and can represent satanic influences. Pray over everything that comes into your homes. Bind any spirits and/or curses that might have been put on them at their place or origin. The old dragon (Satan) works in ways unbeknownst to normal people. Check your homes regarding everything and see if anything pertains to the enemy. Get rid of the things that are not godly, and don't pass them onto unsuspecting individuals. You are just passing those curses on to others. Woe to all who participate in the worship of idols and anything that keeps you from serving your *Lord and Savior*. Some items may seem to be innocent, but by doing a little research, you may find hidden meanings. Christians, *I* want your lives to represent your *Lord Jesus Christ*. Remember what was done in the temple with the money changers. You as Christians should do the same in your lives and homes and also your houses of worship. Start housecleaning and see a difference it makes in the lives of everyone.

People of faith, in whom do you put your faith and trust? Is it in people or things of the world, or is it in your *Heavenly Father?* You, *My* people, cannot have it both ways. Your loyalty cannot be in two places. If you will love one, you will hate the other. If you put your trust in the people of the world and let them make decisions for your benefit, you will be disappointed. Put your faith and trust in the one and only one in whom you can trust completely, one who will never let you down nor deceive you in anyway. Some people of faith, while working in the world, seem to put their trust in others. Instead, pray for all who have authority over you. Pray for guidance for them and wisdom for making the rightful decisions in regard to everyone's best interest. Always be in constant prayer or interceding for others that make decisions affecting all people. Now *I* say again, people of faith, where does your faith and trust lie?

DECEMBER 5, 2016

My children, be ye prepared for the fiery darts of the evil one. *He* is manifesting his presence worldwide with different signs and wonders. *He* is the great deceiver, liar, and manipulator of all time. So many of *My* children even those of the Christian faith are being deceived daily by the old dragon himself (Satan). Unbeknownst to some new people of faith the ways of the enemy, he is very cunning and will use anyone or anything to seduce you into his way of thinking. Even some long-time Christians are susceptible to the wiles of the devil. The more you know *My Word*, the more knowledgeable you will be and more prepared. So *I* say to *My* children, be on the defensive at all times. If in doubt about anything, seek *My Holy Word* in prayer and supplication with thanksgiving. Wait for an answer and conformation. It's *My* desire for all mankind to be saved. Yet there are those proclaiming another way to *Heaven* other than through the blood of *My Son* shed on the cross. The enemy will say that there are other ways. Not so! When in doubt, seek out older Christians in faith to explain *My* plan of salvation. There's only one way to Heaven—that is to accept that *My Son* died on the cross for all mankind's sins and to make *Him Lord* of your life. Do not be deceived by any false doctrines.

DECEMBER 7, 2016

To all the lost, those who have ears, let them hear what *the Word of God* is saying. Lost of the world, there is a real *Heaven* and a real hell. Upon your death, your spirit will enter one or the other. For those who have chosen salvation, upon their demise, their spirit will be absent from the body and present with the *Lord*. Whether people believe in *Heaven* or hell, it's their choice. By not believing doesn't make *Heaven* or hell less real. They exist, and one day will be a reality. If only the lost would understand what it is like to have someone to love them and willing to forgive the sins they've committed. With this acceptance, they become a child of the living *God*, guarantees their place in the kingdom of *God*. Refusing to accept the plan of salvation warrants your destiny to hell. Lost souls, wake up and realize there is a real *Heaven* and hell. You choose where you spend eternity!

December 8, 2016

People of all nations, people, are you being drawn into diverse temptations and sin without even knowing it? If something looks too good to be true, then don't partake. People, are you being fooled by everything? There are those who promise all sorts of financial blessings if you would only do what they say. Don't get trapped by false promises that lead to sin. People, if you don't want to be misled, then turn to the one in whom all blessings flow. The deceivers do not want you to seek out information about your issues or problems. They want you to accept their input on all things. Do not take for granted anything that doesn't sound right! Check all things out, and if you really want the truth, not lies of the enemy, then turn to the one true *God* who cannot lie or deceive you. *He* is faithful and just and will accept all who seek *Him* out and ask for forgiveness. Don't take anything for granted!

December 9, 2016

*M*y faithful one, *I* am now beginning to open the doors before you for your messages to become known. They will comfort, warn against the sins of the world, teach, and entice all who will listen. Your messages from *Me* will enlighten some and distress others. These messages are to glorify the *Holy Trinity* and to warn people of all nations to get their oil lamps in order for the coming of the *Lord*. Some will scoff, yet others will make preparations for *My* coming. These words from *God* are to help *My* people to make changes in their lifestyle. In these messages that *I* have put in your mind and heart are to go forth and help all, whether they are lost or are Christians. They are guidelines to make your lives more productive and to bring *My* people to a relationship with the *Creator*. Most of all the, words are to confirm the love *I* have for all mankind!

DECEMBER 10, 2016

People of faith, where does your faith lie? Is it with *God* or with someone or something else? When seeking help for answers to problems or situations, whom do you seek first? Your answer should always be your *Heavenly Father*. In him, you can put all your faith and trust to solve all your maladies. Remember, nothing is impossible for *God*. If *My* people would seek *God* first in all concerns pertaining to themselves, things would progress faster and easier. Most people of faith cannot as *the Word* says, "Humble themselves before anyone." You must be humble and contrite in spirit before *God*. *He* sees all and knows all. *He* knows what you have needed of before you ask. It seems that even Christians sometimes have a problem with humility and meekness. It is not less manly or less of a person to turn all your cares and woes to someone greater than oneself. *God* sees your heart, so put your faith in the one and only *God*!

Christians, in your daily life, are you putting *God* first? Are you trying to accomplish life's problems with your own ability? People of faith, *I* encourage you to acknowledge *Me* first and foremost in everything pertaining to *My* people. When you don't seek *Me* first, it's then that all goes away. *I* cannot implore enough for the children of faith to keep doing everything on their own. Leave important matters in the hands of your *Savior*. This is why nothing is getting accomplished because you are doing things on your own. In your families, proclaim *Me* above all else. Proclaim the faith and trust you have in *Me* to accomplish what looks to others as impossible. Nothing is hard for *Me*. By honoring *Me* above all else, you are saying, "*Lord*, you can handle this and any situation." Then stand back and watch what prayer can do for those who love *God* first and foremost.

Saints of *God*, do you know *Me*? Do you really know *Me*, or is it that you know about *Me* and of *Me*? By reading the Holy Scriptures, you would know of *Me* and *My* teachings. To get to know *Me*, you need to be spending time in *My Holy Presence*. Don't wait until it's too late to hear *Me* say, "*I* know you not." Take heed and get to know your *God* and the plans *He* has for your life. There's more to being a Christian than going to worship services and heading organizations. It's *My* desire for all *My* followers to get to know *Me* and *My* will for all saints. So many individuals are misled by false teachers who profess from *the Word*. There will be many followers of man-made teachings. Let it be known that wide is the gate that leads to destruction, and narrow is the path that leads to *Heaven*. Remember, saints may come in *My* name, but beware, they are wolves in sheep's clothing. Line up all teachings according to *the Word of God*. It's the ultimate authority!

DECEMBER 15, 2016

Believers, *I* cannot declare enough the importance of studying *My Word* and really understanding it. Memorize and retain every *Word* into your entire being. People of the world are constantly making changes in *My* Holy Scriptures to suit themselves and their lifestyles. They are being used out of context to explain their sins away. You cannot, *I* say cannot sin continually and profess going to *Heaven.* This is what some are teaching. They have left out about repentance and seeking forgiveness. Once forgiven, people are to turn away from sin. *I* say, beware of false teachers, prophets that use *My* words for their own advantage. They will profit nothing. Feed yourselves from *the Word* and only *My Word* which was given by inspiration. Don't be swayed or led astray by other teachings. *My Word* is the only way to get on the pathway to *Heaven.* There is no other!

DECEMBER 16, 2016

Saints, for all those who say "*Lord, Lord*" and yet don't follow *My* teachings, they don't interpret *My Holy Word* for good but for their own benefit, like the Pharisees. To be a follower of the *Lord Jesus Christ* means to follow the teachings of the Bible given by inspiration of *God*. The Holy Scriptures is meant to enlighten *My* followers, to comfort, to instill faith, hope, and charity, also to lead people on the road to salvation and a future in *Heaven*. There are those who have distorted *My Words* for their own way of thinking. Saints, do not listen to other's interpretations of *My* precious *Word*. Seek *Me* in prayer when you read the Holy Scriptures, and *My Holy Spirit* will guide you to a new understanding and interpretation of *My* teachings. For those who misinterpret the Holy Scriptures should remember that one day, every knee will bow, and every tongue will confess that *Jesus Christ* is *Lord* of the whole universe.

Christians, during these celebrations of the birth of *My beloved Son*, are you remembering that he's the reason for the season? Go forth, people of faith, and proclaim the birth of the *Savior*. Tell all the people the reason *He* became flesh in the embodiment of a babe. Then *He* grew up and went about proclaiming all the love and kindness, the good news of *His Heavenly Father*. Take heed, people of faith, and go out in your world of sin and corruption confessing that *Jesus Christ* was born in a manger. *He* grew into manhood and travelled all over the region professing *the Word of God. He* suffered many afflictions and was constantly persecuted but remained faithful. Let *His* life and ministry be an example to follow during the celebrations of the birth—Emmanuel, *God* is with us.

*M*y brothers and sisters, do you honor *Me* by setting aside one special day a week for rest and worship? Are your schedules so busy you can't take a day, a week, and just rest in *My Presence*? *My* brothers and sisters, *I* long to share with you the peace, joy, and serenity of *My* kingdom. It's available for all who come and partake of all the attributes of *Heaven*. Come and set aside a day of rest from all your labors. Enjoy a peaceful day and be still and know that *I* am *God*! *I* long for all *My* brothers and sisters to come to *Me* with joy, thanksgiving, praise, and worship. The total reason for a Sabbath day of rest is for your mental and physical health. Let your bodies and minds enjoy a day of nothingness except thoughts of your heavenly brother, spirit and soul. Come and enjoy with *Me* in a day of rest!

DECEMBER 20, 2016

Sorrows of the gospel, are you sowing the seeds of the gospel to all who will listen and then reaping what you have sown? *My people*, sometimes it may seem as though your seeds didn't take root. Other times, you will be surprised by individual words revealing the seeds you planted long ago. Sometimes, the harvest may feel like it's taken a long time. Sowers, don't be slack because some don't believe. Keep on planting seeds of salvation. To all who have ears, let them hear what *the Word of God* is saying. Be forthright and persistent, not giving up or letting the enemy plant his tares of unbelief. Keep spreading *the Word of God* what you have sown. The beliefs far outweigh the effort. It's all worthwhile when the harvest is reaped!

DECEMBER 21, 2016

To the saints of the world, *I* came to earth to show the way to *Heaven*. *I* came to show the people the attributes of *My Father* and your *Father*. *He* and *I* are one. When you saw *Me*, you saw the *Father*. *I* came to your world as a babe wrapped in swaddling clothes. *I* was *the Word of God* made flesh. During *My* earthly ministry, *I* performed many miracles of healing, fed thousands with bread and fishes, taught in the temples, and all in all was about *My Father's* business. *I* came to show the love of *God* to the world and to share *His* teaching and words of wisdom. Some listened and were amazed while others scoffed. There were those who believed that *I* was the *Messiah* while others disagreed. *I* came to your world to serve, not to be served. *I* came to save the lost by offering a plan of salvation. People of this generation, do not get bound up by materialistic items. Turn your eyes toward *Heaven* and receive gifts of worth beyond measure.

*M*y dear friends, do you understand that as *My* friend you can come to *Me* with any of your concerns, problems, decisions, interest, care, and anything that gives you a moment of grief? *I* am here to advise, console, comfort, and altogether best friend when needed. Your earthly friends sometimes will be unfaithful, disloyal, and not understanding. It could be unintentional and sometimes not aware of doing it. You see, when *I* say *I* am your friend who sticks closer than a brother, that is exactly what *I* intend. *I* will never leave nor forsake you. *I* am always willing to listen. All you have to do is to come into *My Presence* and talk to *Me* about your day's events. Then quietly listen to what the *Spirit of God* is saying to your heart. You can confide in *Me* about your innermost desires and concerns. *I* will listen and no way cast you aside.

DECEMBER 23, 2016

Believers, I've spoken many times in many ways of forgiveness. Some find it easy to forgive a person, especially a brother or sister in faith. Yet while others speak of forgiveness and cannot let go of the hurt afflicted upon them. To forgive totally means to completely forget the harm that has been done to you. Remember it no longer. The one being forgiven needs to stop inflecting pain and hurt on others. Seek out the *Lord* and ask *Him* to help in starting anew. Sometimes irreparable damage has been done, but forgiveness when handled with care can accomplish much. Things will never be the same, but there can be peace amongst individuals. All must seek after the *Lord* with all your spirit, body, and soul. If you cannot and truly forgive and set things right and make peace, then call upon a pastor of your faith for assistance. Try approaching the individual first and see the response. It may well be well worth the effort to confront the person. Do it with love and compassion.

DECEMBER 27, 2016

Believers, *I* cannot instill or emphasize enough the importance of knowing the Holy Scriptures. By the knowledge of *My Word*, it will help you to discern what teaching is wrong and what is false. You will have people declaring, "Thus saith the *Lord*." If it's not found in the Holy Scriptures, then disregard it. Some teachings are from man's teaching and claim to represent *the Word of God* but do nothing to further the kingdom. Those, too, should be disregarded. Evaluate all teachings; just don't assume they are found in the Bible. This is why it's so important to know *My Word*. So believers, devour *My* teachings, sayings, blessing, promises in your spirit. When someone reveals something, you will know whether it is of *God*. *My* faithful believers, one day, you will be richly blessed for your perseverance and dedication to *the Word of God*. Remain diligent and true.

DECEMBER 28, 2016

Christians! Stop! Look! And listen! Stop participating in the things that don't bring you closer to your *Heavenly Father*. Look at all the sins around you. There's sexual perversion, adultery, murders, other assorted sins. Listen to your inner man, and *He* will lead and guide you on the right pathway to *Heaven*. Stop and behold the glories of your *Lord*. Look at all the blessing that has been given to you, a beautiful sunrise and sunset. In seasons, there will be flowers blooming, birds chirping, and trees bowing to the breath of *God*. Listen, *My* children, what the *Spirit* is saying. Discern what the teachings of the world are saying. *My* sheep will know *My* voice. Stop speaking evil of anyone. Remember, all humankind is created by *God*. By speaking unkindly of *God's* creations, you are insulting him. Look for all good in all *My* creations. Listen for any signs of repentance and be ready to lead an individual to the *Lord* and the kingdom of *Heaven*. Watch for any opportunity to speak of the *Lord* and life's plan of salvation.

Saints, are you acting wisely or foolishly? Are you getting prepared and making yourself ready for the coming of your *Lord and Savior*? Being wise in the sight of the *Lord* is being prepared. Being foolish is delaying preparations, saying the *Lord* won't come today. When you are wise, you are always ready and making use of the talents the *Lord* has given you. Every saint has been given gifts or talents of one kind or another. How a person uses them differentiates the foolish from the wise. The talents *I* speak of are your intellect, your abilities to do things for others, helping those in need. By helping the least of these, you are helping *Me*. Your talents regardless of what they may be are to be used to further the kingdom of *God*. The use of your talents whether monetary, helpfulness, prayer, or all-around caring and compassion are gifts from the *Lord*. Some people cannot get out and do things that others do. So their talent could be to befriend a shut-in, to pray in intercession for those hurting. Some can cook meals for those that are hungry. All *My* saints are to use the blessings from the *Lord*, to bless others. If you hoard your blessings and talents for a later use, you may lose out or lose them altogether.

Followers of *Jesus Christ*, there will be times you should remain silent, and there will be instances for you to speak boldly of *the Word of God*. Do not be ashamed to speak of or about your *Lord and Savior*. Be in tuned to the prompting of the *Holy Spirit* in regard when to speak and when to be silent. There are too many of *My* followers today that are embarrassed to speak of their faith. It's like you shouldn't talk about it in public. This is a big problem because *My* followers should be so joyful and thankful. It's because of their salvation and their relationship with the *Lord* that they can't wait to share with loved ones. This problem of remaining silent about their faith is nationwide and worldwide. Others speak out in regard to their rights. They are very bold in this regard, yet mention faith and they will respond, "We don't talk about it publicly." This is very wrong. If more of *My* followers would speak out and let all know what they believe and what they stand for, it could and would make a difference. You have individuals standing up for the rights of others regarding the right to worship, the right to choose a mate, and yet Christians have no rights when it comes to their faith and beliefs. *My* people have a *God*-given right to speak of their *Heavenly Father*, to speak of their faith without being persecuted or defamed in any way. It's up to the followers of the *Lord Jesus Christ* to regain that right and use it for the glory of *God*.

Nonbelievers, when *I* died upon the cross and said "It is finished," that's what it meant. Everything was accomplished on the cross by *My* death. *I* died for all sins to be forgiven, and with the stripes afflicted on *My* back when you become a follower, you are healed! There is nothing more for *Me* to do. It's already been done. People of faith will accept what has already been accomplished! *I* was made a sacrificial *Lamb* for all. It's up to the individual whether or not they accept what has been done. By accepting what *I* have done on the cross means you will become *My* people. Do not be ashamed of *My* name and what *I* sacrificed for all. It was freely given, the most precious gift of all when *God* allowed *His* beloved *Son Jesus* to suffer and die for all to be saved and that none should perish.

D orothy and her husband Joe Mattingly reside in a small town in southern Indiana. Joe is a member of the Catholic church, while Dorothy belongs to an Assembly of God Church. Together they have six children and seven grandchildren.

CPSIA information can be obtained
at www.ICGtesting.com
Printed in the USA
LVHW011737180219
607899LV00003B/566/P

9 781644 160244